Also from Indigo Sea Press
Novels by Nichole R. Bennett

Ghost Mountain

indigoseapress.com

Sleeping Bear

By

Nichole R. Bennett

Stiletto Books
Published by Indigo Sea Press
Winston-Salem

Stiletto Books
Indigo Sea Press, LLC
302 Ricks Drive
Winston-Salem, NC 27103

Copyright 2014 by Nichole R. Bennett

First Stiletto Books edition published
December, 2015
Stiletto Books, Moon Sailor, and all production design are trademarks of Indigo Sea Press, used under license.
For information regarding bulk purchases of this book, digital purchase and special discounts, please contact the publisher at indigoseapress.com

Cover design by Jennifer Blake

Manufactured in the United States of America
ISBN 978-1-63066-361-2

To Douglas County Deputy Sheriff (Retired) Jim Westcott,
Who was always available to help me with scenarios and made sure I
was as accurate as possible.
I love you, Dad.

Prologue

Robert ran his hand through his wind-blown hair. One of his favorite things about South Dakota was the lack of a helmet law. The wind blowing through his hair as he rode his Fat Boy was one of the most liberating feelings he'd ever felt. It was much better than back home where he had to wear a helmet just to ride around the block.

The mild roar of distant motorcycles penetrated the peaceful silence of Bear Butte. It was only the first day of the weeklong Black Hills Motorcycle Classic and Robert had seen all he wanted to. Home–and the stable, rut-like life he'd forged there–was looking better all the time.

I should head home tomorrow. Coming here had been a mistake. He missed his wife and son. And the miles on the bike hadn't been as easy on his back and butt now that he was approaching his 40s as those same miles had been decades earlier.

Stupid mid-life crisis. Robert chuckled.

In the distance, Robert could see the VA Medical Center, the parking lot almost empty as sunset started to approach. Most of the bikers were headed to the campgrounds where music's superstars would be performing. Some of the best outdoor concerts in the world took place at the annual event. Robert had done his best to avoid the crowds, preferring the solitude of the ride to the thumping bass of the guitars.

It gave him plenty of time to think about the fight he'd had with his wife. He should call Ellen and apologize, but the idea of groveling wasn't appealing. Even if she had been right. He had been keeping things from her. If nothing else, the trip had given him time to think.

"Hey, man. Long time, no see."

Robert stiffened as he recognized the voice. He hadn't expected to see anyone who knew him here. The ride over from Washington State for the Black Hills Motorcycle Classic had been a last minute decision made after another argument with Ellen. The impromptu trip to see Bear Butte even less planned. Then again, this was a Mecca for motorcyclists from all walks of life. Robert stepped off his motorcycle and turned to look at the man who was speaking. "Yeah. I guess it has."

"Dude, you know it has. I'd ask what you've been up to, but it doesn't really matter. I don't really care."

"You never were one for small talk, if I remember right." Robert couldn't remember the man's name. Vacuum? Villain? Viper, maybe? Something that started with a V. It didn't matter, really. Robert wasn't interested in renewing the man's acquaintance.

He locked his bike, stuck the key in his pocket and turned toward the trail heading up the Butte.

"Bear! I'm talking to you! Or don't you go by that anymore?"

"Man, I haven't used that name in years," Robert replied. "It's Robert now. Sometimes Bob or Bobby."

"Don't matter none to me. You'll always be Bear." The other man looked Robert up and down. "You can change all you want on the outside. Don't mean nothing. You're still the same. You're still Bear."

Robert chuckled. "Nah. It's been like twenty years. Everyone changes. Even you."

Robert scrutinized the other man long enough to see a resemblance, but decided the years must not have been easy for the other man. He was also dressed in worn jeans and a black t-shirt advertising a past motorcycle classic. He looked much older than Robert had remembered him, but the features were there. A few more scars. A lot more lines. *But it's been over twenty years,* he reminded himself. *And they obviously haven't all been good years for....*

No matter how lousy Robert was with names, he couldn't deny the family resemblance. He'd been trying to forget for more than two decades.

"No, Bear. I haven't changed." The man took a few steps closer to Robert and spit, the wad of slobber landing between Robert's feet. "And I don't believe you have either. You're gonna pay for what you done."

2

"Look, it was a long time ago. I was there, yeah. But I didn't do anything. Maybe that was my mistake." Robert took a few steps back, his hands raised to show that he held no malice. "I turned my life around, man. I was pretty messed up back then. I've been trying to make amends."

The scowl that formed on the other man's face told Robert his words had fallen on deaf ears. Robert searched his brain again for the other man's name, but came up blank. Nor could he remember the name of the man's brother. The brother who's untimely and preventable death seemed to have festered such venomous feelings.

"Well…umm…it's been great seeing ya. Take care. Ride safe." Robert turned to head up the trail toward Bear Butte's summit.

"Bear," the other man called.

Robert turned around and felt the punch to his jaw before he could even register the man's flying fist.

"I suppose I deserved that." Robert regarded his attacker with a mixture of wariness and pity.

"You deserve more than that," the other man calmly stated before throwing a second punch, this one a direct hit to the solar plexus causing Robert to stumble back and knocking the wind out of him. "Not so tough anymore, are ya?"

Robert saw the man's boot raise, and felt the sickening crunch when the boot connected with Robert's unprotected rib cage. Out of breath and out of practice, Robert thought of nothing except avoiding the next kick.

After what seemed an eternity, the beating stopped. His attacker knelt down, grabbed Robert's shirt and pulled him to a semi-sitting position. Robert could see his own blood splattered on the man in front of him.

"You deserve a lot more." The venom in the man's voice was unmistakable. "A lot more."

Robert felt the cold metal slide swiftly in and out of his side. He didn't feel any pain until he saw the knife his attacker held. Then the pain and shock hit him so hard Robert wasn't sure if it was real or a result of realizing the stab wound should hurt. Because of the extent of his injuries, Robert was finding it difficult to breathe.

Maybe I can still get out of this, he thought. Aloud he said, "Hey man, I know you're angry…"

Robert couldn't say another word as he watched his attacker bring the knife toward Robert's neck.

He never felt the blade, now warm and sticky with Robert's own blood, slice his carotid artery and windpipe.

Death came quickly.

Chapter One

I was irritable. It had to be at least one hundred degrees in the shade and it wasn't even noon yet. The population of Western South Dakota had increased by one hundred thousand almost overnight and probably ninety percent of them were riding motorcycles that sounded like they really needed new mufflers.

The annual Black Hills Motorcycle Classic had been in full swing for barely twenty-four hours—an event someone can't fully appreciate until they've lived through one.

I didn't usually suffer from road rage, but something about the influx of bodies and the muffled rumble of the motorcycles shaking everything seemed to put me on edge. Of course, the cacophony of three young, excited children in the back seat probably didn't help matters, either. I was determined not to let anything bother me.

Success was out of reach.

My kids had wanted to go swimming, but even the local pools seemed to have more people than water in them. To keep my son and twin daughters occupied—and my sanity intact—I had decided to take the three to a nearby lake we'd found earlier in the summer. I planned to spend a fun-filled day with eight-year-old Zach and his six-year-old sisters, Mackenzie and Madison, swimming, playing on the small, sand-covered beach, and hiking in the surrounding woods.

Roubaix Lake, mere minutes from Rapid City, was a beautiful, and serene place to escape from the stress of everyday life, a jewel mostly-undiscovered by the thousands of tourists currently in the area. Hidden in the Black Hills between Nemo and Deadwood, cell phone reception in the area was sketchy at best. It's an area where "can you hear me now?" became more than an advertising slogan.

We were almost to the point of total blackout, when my cell phone rang.

Assuming it was my husband, Matt, on the other end, I didn't bother with hellos. "Honey, we're almost at the lake and I'm not sure how much longer I'll have reception."

5

The initial silence on the other end was the first indication I wasn't speaking to Matt.

"Mrs. Baker? Cerri? It's Joe Oliver."

He didn't need to introduce himself. FBI Special Agent Joseph Oliver's voice hadn't changed since I'd last spoken to him. I met Agent Oliver the previous fall when I accidentally got mixed up in a murder investigation. I couldn't imagine why he'd be contacting me now since the killer had been caught was awaiting trial. At the time I was sure the entire experience fell under the karmic category of "no good deed goes unpunished," but the preceding eleven months had given me a slightly less jaded view of the circumstances surrounding the event.

But only slightly.

I pulled my SUV onto the shoulder of the road before responding. "Agent Oliver. How nice to hear from you. Unfortunately, I'm a little busy today." I hoped my voice had the proper mixture of politeness and professional coolness that would give Agent Oliver the message that I was too busy for whatever he needed. Today and every day.

"Cerri, I'm sorry to bother you, but I have a … situation that requires your … talents."

My stomach dropped as if I'd just received terrible news. Agent Oliver didn't need to expound on his statement. The memory of our last encounter came rushing back.

When we first moved to Cogan Ridge, a suburb of Rapid City, my Lakota spirit guide decided to make an appearance. When a murder took place at Devil's Tower, He Who Waits wouldn't leave me alone until I shared the information he gave me with the authorities. Of course, that put me at the top of Agent Oliver's suspect list until I could prove my innocence.

Proving my innocence, however, required me to resort to the very practices and traditions I'd spent my life trying to escape. I didn't believe in the old-religion, hocus-pocus, mumbo-jumbo my mother and sister embraced. It was a difficult legacy to overcome, since I was the one named Cerridwen, after the pre-Christian Celtic goddess who was said to have prophetic powers and divine knowledge. Even shortening my name to Cerri—pronounced like Carrie—didn't help. I knew what the name meant.

My sister lucked out with the name Wendy.

Agent Oliver interrupted my thoughts. "Cerri, are you there? Have I lost you?"

"Umm, yeah, still here . . . Sorry. Umm, I don't know how I can help." Zach began wiggling around to torment his sisters, causing me to give him a warning look. "Besides, the kids and I are headed to the lake for the day."

"So I understand," Agent Oliver replied, with a touch of amusement. I wasn't used to his voice being anything except stern. "I'll be at your place tomorrow morning around ten." There was no good-bye as he hung up.

An involuntary growl of frustration escaped my lips as I snapped my phone shut and tossed it into the beach bag sitting on the passenger's seat.

"Are we still going to the lake, Mommy?" Kenzie asked from the backseat.

"Of course, honey," I replied as I pulled back on the road.

Whatever supernatural help Agent Oliver needed would have to wait.

Chapter Two

The rest of the day passed uneventfully. Or as uneventfully as possible while being preoccupied with the fact the FBI was planning to show up at your door the following day.

I wasn't sure if being warned was a good thing. I had a tendency to obsess over things I had no control over and a visit from the FBI qualified as worthy for obsession.

Zach, Maddie, and Kenzie swam, built sand castles, and caught minnows and toads. We even hiked around the lake where the kids played a game of hide and seek through the surrounding woods.

After tiring the three of them out at Roubaix Lake, we grabbed some burgers from a fast food place on the way home and pulled in the drive just after Matt.

Matt, an associate professor of geology at South Dakota's School of Mines and Technology, taught classes year round. He tried to instill a love of rocks in the minds of young co-eds. It was not an attitude he'd managed to share with me, though. I didn't find rocks that exciting.

I preferred writing to science, so my job as a freelance writer was the perfect fit for me. It let me schedule work commitments around my family obligations and gave me plenty of time for my various hobbies.

Despite our main interests lying in different areas, Matt and I shared almost everything else. We both loved the outdoors and, honestly, we both liked to read. Though he preferred non-fiction to the mind-escaping novels I always selected.

Most importantly, we enjoyed spending time with our kids and each other. I couldn't have asked for more.

No matter what was going on in our lives, the two of us made it a habit to share our day's events while we washed and dried the dinner dishes. Even though we had a dishwasher and even when the dishes consisted mainly of paper bags and burger wrappers.

Matt had already heard the highlights of the day from the kid's perspective. Zach excitedly relayed chasing Maddie with a toad, Maddie told her dad about the sand castle the girls built, and Kenzie gave a play-by-play of the hide and seek game. I stayed quiet through dinner hoping Matt didn't notice how preoccupied I was.

"I'm not sure who looks forward to the end of a semester more, students or teachers," Matt began. "I would have much rather spent the day with you guys at the lake."

"That's nice, honey." I wasn't really listening, but Matt had paused, so I was pretty sure I should say something.

"So I decided to quit my job and tomorrow I'll run off with my secretary."

"Oh, okay," I said. "Hey! What did you say?"

Matt chuckled. "Yeah, I didn't think you were listening. Want to tell me what's up? The kids give you a bad time today? It sounded like they had a great time."

I sighed and sat down at the table. "They did. The kids were great. I think Kenzie might have a little sunburn on her shoulders. She didn't stay still long enough to put much sunscreen on. And Maddie probably has sand everywhere from the size of the castle she was trying to build. Zach spent at least an hour looking for tadpoles. The kids were fine." I paused, not sure how to verbalize what was on my mind.

"So what is it?"

"Agent Oliver called."

A look of confusion passed over his face. "Agent . . . Oh! What did he want?" Matt took a seat across from me and grabbed my hand, waiting patiently for my response.

"He wants to come by here tomorrow. He said he has something he needs my . . . um . . . talents, I think was the word he used . . . to help with."

The talents Agent Oliver wanted to use were the exact ones I barely acknowledged. The women in my family referred to themselves as "wise women." They knew all there was to know about crystals and herbs. Tarot cards were more common than playing cards in the house I grew up in and ghost stories were told as actual events, not saved for scaring people at campfires. As an adult,

I had done everything I could to get as far from those traditions as possible.

It hadn't worked.

Matt looked at me quizzically. "Well? Did he say anything else?"

I shook my head. "Nope. And I couldn't really ask, either. We were almost to the lake when he called. You know how bad the cell reception is out there."

"What are you going to do?"

"That's just it. I don't know. I don't know what he wants. I don't even know if I can help." I lowered my voice to a whisper. "It's not like last time. I haven't *seen* anything."

I didn't have to explain further. Matt knew, and mostly accepted, my family's unique beliefs. He'd even encouraged me to assist the FBI when a man was found murdered at Devils Tower. To tell the truth, though, I'd already gotten involved by the time Matt found out, but he was the one who made me feel better about helping. He even knew about He Who Waits.

And he loved me anyway.

"So no headless horsemen?" Matt asked. "Nobody walking through the walls?"

Just because my husband was supportive didn't mean he wouldn't tease me about it.

"Nope. Nothing." I stood up. "I guess I'll just see what happens tomorrow."

Matt also stood from the table. "I'll go read to the kids. Maybe get them out of your hair for a bit. Something—or *someone*—may come to you."

He left the kitchen pretending to ignore the look I was giving him. The instant he turned the corner to head down the hall, I smelled old leather. I associated the scent with He Who Waits. If I could smell him, I wasn't alone.

"Hello, *Cuwitku*." He Who Waits spoke from behind me. Without turning around, I knew he'd be wearing the same tan-colored suede pants and shirt. The beadwork on the shirt was beautiful, but I'd never asked him what it meant. I knew that his clothing was made of buffalo, but I don't know how I knew it.

10

Probably the same way that I knew *Cuwitku* meant "daughter" without him ever translating.

When I finally turned to face him, I found he hadn't changed. His clothing was as I'd always seen it. His skin still reminded me of tanned leather hue and his salt and pepper hair was collected in a loose braid down his back. Time had not changed He Who Waits. He looked the same now as he did when I was a little girl and thought of him as my imaginary friend. I knew now that he was more than that. He Who Waits was my *Tuwe Ya*, or guide, whether I wanted him or not. Based on research I'd done online, I'd come to believe he was probably a shaman or medicine man. Whatever else he was, was a mystery to me.

"I guess you already know about the phone call, don't you?" It was a rhetorical question. He Who Waits seemed to know everything.

"I know you are once again being called to help someone find justice," came his reply.

I rolled my eyes. "Great. It probably won't be easy this time, either."

"The right things often are not the easy things, Cerridwen. You teach your children that. It is the way of things."

As much as I hated to admit it, he was right. I sat back down at the table. From the basement, I could hear Matt reading the *Wizard of Oz*, using different voices for the characters. I knew from experience that all three kids would be sitting, listening to their dad's rendition.

"So what do I do?"

"You do what you must to fulfill your destiny, *Cuwitku*. Is there another option?"

"This isn't my thing," I started to protest. "Can't someone else help? I'm not a cop."

Experience told me this was a pointless argument. It didn't work last time and wouldn't work now. For a brief moment I wondered if He Who Waits was getting as frustrated at me as I did when Zach tried pushing an issue.

"You are just unsure of yourself. Uncertain of the outcome and dislike the idea of being not the one in control. You must learn to accept your destiny. It is part of the journey."

I sighed. "Okay. Tell me what you know about this and I'll try to help."

The shaman nodded, as if he expected that I would concede. "There is much I do not know. Another desecration has taken place at another sacred site."

"What? Again? How many sacred sites are there?" He Who Waits lured me into helping the FBI last time because the murder took place on Lakota Holy Ground.

"All Earth is sacred, *Cuwitku.* In the *Paha Sapa*, there are many *Waka Oyanke*."

Paha Sapa was the Lakota phrase for the Black Hills. I figured that *Waka Oyanke* must mean a sacred place.

"So something happened at a different sacred place this time? Gotcha. What do want me to do? Wait. Let me guess. You want me to help get justice for the victim, right?" I knew I sounded snotty, but I couldn't seem to help myself. I've always preferred my mysteries in paperback, not real life.

He Who Waits solemnly nodded once, effectively ignoring my rudeness.

"How exactly am I supposed to do that?"

The look on the medicine man's face told me either he didn't have the answer or he wouldn't have told me if he did. Not that I expected anything else, but I had to try.

"Sometimes I really wish you would give me real answers to questions, you know?"

He Who Waits refused to respond.

In fact, he wasn't even there anymore.

Chapter Three

True to his word, Agent Oliver pulled in the drive promptly at ten. I didn't want the kids around while I talked with him, so I sent them across the street where Bobbi and Meghan, a set of teenage sisters, were available to baby sit for an hour or so. Zach, Maddie, and Kenzie rode the school bus with the older girls and seemed to really like them. Bobbi and Meghan were great with the kids, too.

I didn't give Agent Oliver the opportunity to knock, opening the door as soon as he reached it. "Come on in," I invited, leading the way to the living room.

Agent Oliver looked much the same as he had when I'd last seen him. He was built like a professional football player, or a brick wall. His dirty blond hair was cut in its usual "high and tight" and his steel-grey eyes reminded me of the gun I knew he carried in his shoulder holster. I knew why he was here—sort of—so his physical appearance wasn't as daunting as the first time he'd shown up at my door. I probably would have found him handsome if he didn't intimidate me so much.

I led Agent Oliver to the living room. He sat in the recliner and I took a seat on the couch. Full of nervous energy, he tapped his foot in a steady rhythm. As I watched, he began to rub his left palm with his right thumb. During the moments when his foot ceased moving, he seemed to rub even harder making me doubt he was aware of the movement. I waited for him to say something, to explain his presence.

Finally, I couldn't stand the silence anymore. "You said you needed my help. I'm not sure what I can do…"

Agent Oliver shifted uneasily in the chair. His eyes darted a bit, adding to his look of discomfort. "Look, my bosses don't know I'm here."

"Really?" I was surprised. "Didn't they kind of force you to work with me last time?" That wasn't exactly true. To be more accurate, my mother had convinced my father that I could help since

13

I was getting information from He Who Waits anyway. Since Dad's retirement from the military, he—like a number of Army Generals before him—had gone to work for some government spy agency. A few well-placed phone calls moved me from suspect number one to consultant. To say Agent Oliver hadn't been pleased with my overnight change in status was putting it lightly.

"Yeah, well, this time I'm here on my own."

"So you said, Agent Oliver."

"Call me 'Joe', please, Mrs. Baker."

That was a twist. When I'd worked with Agent Oliver—I mean, Joe—before, he could barely bring himself to call me 'Mrs. Baker.' I wasn't sure what had brought about his change of heart, but I decided to let it go.

"Well, then, call me 'Cerri.' But I still don't see how I can help.

Joe sighed deeply. "This isn't easy for me..."

I could see that. "Why don't you start with why you think I could help?"

He cleared his throat. "Look, what I'm going to tell you is in confidence. Once I explain what I know, what I need, then maybe you will understand why I'm here."

I nodded and repeated, "Why don't you start with why you think I could help?"

"First, because of the location of the crime."

"Devils Tower?" The murder I helped solve before had taken place at our country's first National Monument. Since the visit from He Who Waits the night before, I knew whatever brought Joe here probably didn't happen at that site, but he did seem to need some encouragement to tell me anything more. I briefly wondered if he had trust issues or control issues making it so difficult for him to get to the point. Then again, maybe it was the cop in him. Either way, I was grateful for my training as a freelance journalist which made getting information out of this private man a little easier.

"No, another place. This time Bear Butte...it's another landmark, another Lakota Holy Site." Joe studied my face, as if searching for a reaction.

I knew about Bear Butte, of course. It was one of the few

14

geological formations breaking up the scenery between Rapid City and the Wyoming State line. I'd been meaning to take the kids hiking there since it wasn't so far from town that stopping for a bathroom brake would be unreasonable.

The more I thought about the site, though, the more something seemed familiar. It occurred to me that I'd heard something about it on the news recently and said as much to Joe.

He looked almost relieved that I mentioned it. "I'm sure you did. Two nights ago there was a shooting there. Some members of an outlaw biker gang, here for the motorcycle classic, were causing some problems. They were basically taking over the area around the Butte, starting with the campground."

Joe pulled a notebook out of his suit pocket, opened it and quickly scanned a page. "A rival gang tried challenging them, trying to move in on their drug business, we think," he continued. "A few off-duty officers from other states were also in the area at the time. They were actually vacationing here, also for the classic. When the two rival gangs started going at each other, the off-duty officers tried to break it up."

He paused, again watching my face to judge any reaction. He was back in investigator mode and seemed less nervous as he relayed the facts without emotion. "At some point during the fight, somebody pulled a gun. Right now the details of who fired the first shot are a bit sketchy, but that's beside the point. In the process of the gun fight, two men died and three were injured, including one of the off-duty officers."

"Sounds like you have that case wrapped up. Why do you need my help?"

"When our forensics team processed the scene, they found another victim."

"Someone was caught in the cross fire?"

Joe shifted a bit in his seat, telling me we were back in uncomfortable territory.

"No. I mean, not exactly."

I waited for him to continue. Part of me enjoyed watching the FBI agent squirm as I remembered how I felt under his scrutiny.

Joe took a deep breath before speaking. "Yes, there was a bullet wound. But it didn't bleed."

Again, Joe watched my face to gauge my reaction. A bullet wound that didn't bleed sounded pretty far-fetched to me, until....

"Wait. That means he was already dead."

Joe nodded. "Exactly. His throat had been sliced, Guy was pretty beat up, too. He was obviously killed before the incident the other night, but the medical examiner said it was probably only a few hours before."

We fell into another silent pause.

"So that guy wasn't part of the gang fight at all, was he? He was killed first and you don't know why do you." I was stalling, thinking aloud in an effort to wrap my head around the issue. As a freelance journalist, it was a technique I'd used often when interviewing experts.

Again, Joe nodded. I learned last time I worked with him that he was a man of few words.

Ever since we began talking, something had bothered me. Finally, I was able to discern it. "Wait, isn't Bear Butte a state park? Why would the FBI even be involved?"

In all my dealings with Joe, I'd never seen him let his guard down. He was a professional through and through. That's why the guilty look that crossed his face came as such a shock to me.

"I have a friend who's a ranger out there. He and I go way back," the agent explained. "Yes, it is state land, but we were called in originally for the extra help. Maybe you haven't noticed, but there are a lot more people in the Black Hills right now."

His sarcasm wasn't lost on me, but I remained quiet.

"When the shooting took place, just about every law enforcement agency in the area sent whatever extra manpower they could spare. When I got there, though, I knew something wasn't right with this body. I talked to my buddy out there, Tommy King, and he gave me the details."

I let his words sink in a bit before I responded.

"I guess I'm still not sure what you want me to do."

"I'll be honest with you, I'm not sure either." For the first time, I

16

noticed the bags forming under Joe's steel-grey eyes. He looked tired, slightly worried even. "I was hoping, maybe, that you had some ... insight on this case?"

It was a question, not a statement. One I didn't know how to answer.

I suppose I could have said something like "Sorry, no spirits or ghosts showing up here telling me major facts about this murder, but thanks for asking," but I wasn't sure that would make either of us feel better. Instead I remained quiet.

Joe must have realized what my silence meant. "Nothing, huh?"

"I'm sorry," I replied.

His sigh spoke volumes. "Well, it was worth a try, right?"

"Yeah, I guess so. I'm sorry, Joe. I just don't know anything about it." Well, that wasn't completely true, but I didn't have anything worth telling, either.

Joe stood up and started toward the door. I followed, not knowing what to say. When I finally did speak, Joe started at the same time.

"I'll let you know—" I began.

"If you think of anything—" he started.

"Sorry, you go ahead," I said after we'd both abruptly stopped speaking.

"I was just going to say that if you think of anything or hear anything that might help, I'd really appreciate it." Joe still looked nervous, as if it were difficult for him to ask for help.

"I will. I mean, I'm not sure if I will ... learn anything that will help, but if I do, I will call."

"That's all I can ask for." Joe handed me a business card, very similar to the one he'd given me the first time he arrived on my doorstep. This one, though, had a cell phone number written in blue ink below his name. "Call my cell. It's probably easier than trying to reach me at the office. And, Cerri, thank you."

With that, he turned and left.

Chapter Four

My kids came barreling through the door a few minutes later. After making lunches and refereeing a squabble between Zach and Kenzie, who was often the recipient of her brother's torment, I was ready for some quiet time, even if the kids weren't. For a brief moment I missed the days when the three were guaranteed to take an afternoon nap.

Instead of a nap, I asked them each to play quietly for a bit. It was too hot to be outside, with the temperatures once again climbing into the triple digits. Maddie decided to read, Kenzie opted to draw, and Zach begged for some time on the computer playing a game his dad had recently bought. We had an older computer in the family room not connected to the Internet for the kids to use for games.

Having the children occupied gave me time to do some work for Joe.

Experience had taught me that He Who Waits wouldn't show up just because I wanted him to. But since our last crime-fighting encounter, I'd been trying to learn to *summon* him. Well, maybe *summon* wasn't exactly what I was doing, but I was determined to find a way to call him when I needed him. If for nothing else than to make me feel better.

I headed into my office. As a freelance journalist, I had procured one of the bedrooms in our four-bedroom Craftsman-style bungalow to use as a combination an office and craft room – my own private sanctuary for work and play. In addition to a desk and laptop computer, I had an all-in-one scanner, printer, copier, and fax as well as numerous bookcases stuffed to the brim. It was also a place to store the tools and supplies of my many hobbies: soap making, candle making, sewing, and knitting. As much as I enjoyed crafts, I sometimes thought I was born a generation or two late. I kept a few candles and a deck of Tarot cards in there, as well. Originally, they served as reminders of my past. Lately, though, I'd actually been reverting more to the things I'd learned as a child. The amateur psychologist in me made a note to do some serious analyzing about my childhood regressions later.

I shut the door to my office, making sure to keep it open a few inches so I could hear the kids if they decided to get into mischief. I took out one of the white candles I'd bought weeks earlier. After a short prayer, I lit the candle, asking He Who Waits to make his presence known. I knew I'd seen my mother do similar things when I was growing up, but I couldn't remember her exact methods. Rather than suffering through a lecture from Ma, I took what I remembered and combined it with some pointers I'd gleaned through an Internet search. The result was as jumbled as I felt.

"Hello, *Cuwitku*," came the shaman's deep voice.

I was so surprised to hear the sound I almost screamed. Honestly, I hadn't believed it would work.

"You knew it would work, Cerridwen. That is why you tried."

"Well, yeah," I said, sheepishly. "I didn't think it would work."

He Who Waits chuckled. "*Niye on cikala wowicala.*"

That was a new phrase, one I didn't understand. Confusion must have shown on my face.

"You are with little faith," he explained. "All things are connected. To get aid from a source, you must only ask. However, the source of assistance is not always expected."

Inhaling deeply, I struggled to find the words to begin. "Okay," I finally started, "the FBI wants my help. Again."

He Who Waits nodded, urging me to continue.

"Someone was killed at Bear Butte the other day. Agent Oliver thinks you can give me some information to help find the killer." I paused, hoping the shaman would decide to give me all the details and we'd be done with this. The extended silence told me that wasn't going to be the case, but I had to try anyway. "Can you?"

I hadn't expected an answer and wasn't surprised when one wasn't forthcoming.

Finally, I couldn't stand the silence any longer. "Okay, so is there anything you can tell me? Anything that can help?"

"I have told you before, it is your *ozuye* to see justice done." Once again He Who Waits opted to remind me that my destiny was

19

to help people.

"I'm starting to understand that," I replied. "My problem is I'm not sure how. I don't know where to start."

He Who Waits looked confused. "You must start at the beginning, of course."

I started to say something smart-alecky, when a bang from the other room distracted me. It sounded as if one of the girls was getting something out of their closet. "You girls be careful, okay?" I yelled.

"Okay, Mommy," came Maddie's voice.

To He Who Waits I said, "Seriously, I have no idea where to start. I'm not a cop, remember? At least the last time you gave me information to start with. Can't you do that again?"

Previously, He Who Waits had given me many of the details of the crime before I ever contacted the FBI. Was it too much to ask for the same information this time?

"Often times, you must search for the *ayu pte* you seek."

Another phrase I didn't understand. This was going nowhere fast.

I tried repeating the phrase, but butchered the pronunciation.

He Who Waits seemed to struggle for the correct English word. Finally, he spoke. "Answer. You must search for the answer you seek."

Great. I wasn't getting any more information in English then I was in He Who Wait's native Lakota language.

"Do you have a name? Anything for me to start with?"

Giggles and gibberish came from the girls' room. It sounded like they were probably playing a game. Like many twins, Maddie and Kenzie shared a secret language no one else was privy to. They usually reserved it for annoying their brother or chatting alone in their room.

The shaman waited for the giggles to die down before replying, which I thought strange because I didn't think anyone else could hear him. "I have nothing for you now. First you must start to find the information. Start with the history of *Mato Paha.*"

With that, He Who Waits left my office by disappearing into thin air.

Chapter Five

The rest of the day passed by uneventfully.

By mid-afternoon, I decided I should start thinking about dinner. It was much too hot to cook indoors and I didn't want to go to the store, since that would require going outside to get into the car. Burgers on the grill sounded like the perfect meal.

I was almost finished preparing a salad to accompany the burgers by the time Matt got home.

After changing into more comfortable—and cooler—clothes, Matt got the grill going and dinner was on the table in no time.

Dinner at the Baker house was always a family affair. The kids helped make it and Matt helped with clean up. During the actual meal, conversation was designed to include every member of the family. Days were reported on, current events were discussed. I made a conscious effort, though, to avoid talking about anything in the "hocus-pocus" arena.

When the meal was finished, Matt and I excused the kids, who ran off to play a board game. Not for the first time, I was grateful that our kids were all such good friends and enjoyed playing together. It made my job as a mom so much easier.

I could hear the kids setting up the game in the living room as Matt started to clear the table. Even though the house had come with a dishwasher, it was rarely used. The nightly ritual of cleaning up after dinner was the time Matt and I used to catch up on our day and discuss the things we chose not to mention in front of the kids.

That was the time of day I discussed the hocus-pocus with my scientific-minded husband. And it wasn't always pretty.

After hearing about his day, which consisted mostly of lecturing classes, he asked me what Joe had wanted. As best I could, I filled Matt in on Joe's visit as well what little information I had learned from He Who Waits. I finished my tale just as the last dish was dried and put into the cupboard.

"Wow. Not much to go on, huh?" he asked, sitting down at the table.

I sat next to him. "Nope. I'm really not even sure where to start."

"You were told to start at the beginning, huh?" Matt repeated the phrase He Who Waits had spoken earlier. "What do you think that means?"

It still didn't spark any brilliant ideas and I said as much.

I could tell Matt was thinking. He started running his hand through his light brown hair, massaging the back of his skull. His blue eyes focused on the far wall, as if the answer would mysteriously appear if only he stared long enough. It was a look I'd seen many times before as he contemplated a difficult decision.

"Start at the beginning." He repeated the phrase two or three times as I waited in silence. "The beginning of Bear Butte, maybe?"

It was as good an idea as any other. "Maybe. I guess it couldn't hurt to find out more about it, right? Maybe the legend behind it? Knowing the legend of Devils Tower didn't help last time, though."

"No, but you had more to go on then. You had a name last time." Matt was silent again. "Is it possible your guide doesn't know the victim's name? The other guy was from around here, right? Maybe this guy is in town for the Motorcycle Classic and that has something to do with the lack of information."

On the surface, it seemed like a logical explanation. But it didn't answer my question as to how I could be of any help to Joe.

"Find out what you can about Bear Butte. Maybe you can figure out why the guy was there," Matt suggested. "By then, maybe Joe will have something more for you to go on. Or maybe your guide can look the dead guy up in the 'newly deceased directory'."

I gave Matt a half-hearted smile at his lame idea of a joke. "Okay," I finally said. "You might be right. I'll find out what I can about Bear Butte and see where that gets me. Maybe I can use my cards to see if that helps."

I hadn't told Matt that I'd used the Tarot cards to help me contact He Who Waits earlier that afternoon. Despite how far I'd come, I was still embarrassed about that part of my heritage.

Matt nodded and stood up from the table where he'd sat. He leaned over and kissed the top of my head before heading toward the living room. "I'm going to check on our three and make sure no one's cheating." Matt was loud enough for the kids to hear, eliciting a chorus of accusations, denials and laughter.

My favorite sounds in the world were the laughter of Zach, Maddie, and Kenzie.

The sound of my children and husband enjoying their time together was a nightly occurrence. I was grateful for each of my wonderful kids and for their attentive father. I said a quick prayer of gratitude as I headed back toward my office.

Okay, so I was getting sappy. It was a diversion to keep from researching this latest murder. I knew that, but the realization didn't make me move any faster.

Once in the office, I turned on my computer. I planned to start looking up information on Bear Butte, but the unmistakable "ping" of an instant message diverted me. My sister, Wendy, was very much like our mother—pure pit bull. I knew I wouldn't be getting much research done. At least until Wendy had a chance to tell me what it was that she wanted to say.

"Guess what?" Wendy's yellow-colored text was hard to read on my screen. As a nine-one-one dispatcher, Wendy spent her work hours on the phone and practically refused to spend her off-duty hours on one. As a result, most of the contact I had with her was via e-mail or instant messages.

"What?"

"I'm getting institutionalized!"

A smile crept across my face. Wendy often teased that marriage was an institution and she never planned to be institutionalized. Those three words could only mean Jack, her long-time beau, had finally broken down her defenses.

"That's great, Wen!" I typed back. "When's the big day?"

As my sister rambled on about various wedding ideas ranging from a pirate-themed ceremony to eloping in Vegas and having Elvis perform the nuptials, I started my research with news reports of the recent days. Thankfully, Wendy's IM ramblings didn't require a lot of response on my part.

Recent news reports about Bear Butte didn't add much beyond what Agent Oliver – Joe – had told me. Most of what I found revolved around the shooting and the biker gang involved, with barely a mention about anybody who was not part of the shootout.

"So what do you think?" Wendy's message forced me back to our conversation and I quickly scanned her last few posts to make sure I wasn't missing something.

"I think you and Jack will be very happy no matter when or where or how you decide to make it official."

"You're no help!"

I rolled my eyes. Even if I'd told Wendy exactly what I thought – that it didn't matter how she and Jack got married as long as they both agreed it or that maybe they should just get married by a justice of the peace – she wouldn't take my advice seriously. Wendy almost never took my advice seriously. I finally asked her, "What does Jack want?"

"Oh, you know him. He doesn't care," she typed. "But he did kinda like the pirate idea."

Jack would. "So go pirate."

Wendy started telling me everything that would go into a pirate-themed wedding, from finding a judge who would be willing to go along with it to creating period-style costumes. When she said she was going to find pictures of some dresses for me look at (pirate dresses, of course), I knew it was safe to return to my research.

Looking for Bear Butte, I found references to a lawsuit filed by members of various tribes calling themselves Protectors of the Black Hills. It was interesting, but not helpful. I bookmarked it for later, in case I needed the information. I did, however, make a mental note to ask Joe about them.

The next site I found gave some history of the butte. I learned that it was established as a state park in 1961 and was an important religious site and landmark to many of the ancient Plains tribes. Many Native Americans still considered the site sacred and left prayer cloths and prayer bundles around the base of the butte and other types of offerings at the top. The name Bear Butte was translated from the Lakota name *Mato Paha*, which meant 'Bear Mountain.' A little more research told me there was camping available nearby and a heard of buffalo made its home near the summit.

Interesting, but not helpful.

I heard a computerized-version of a door shutting. After checking, I verified that Wendy had indeed signed out of the instant message program.

So much for saying good night.

I attributed Wendy's rudeness to a combination of pre-wedding jitters and genetics. Another trait my mother and sister shared was their habit of occasionally ending conversations rather abruptly or not at all.

Having not learned anything that seemed important, I was ready to log off the computer and get the kids into bed. At the last minute, I decided to check my e-mail and found a request from magazine editor Sarah Martin. Sarah and I had gone to college together and while I now supplemented the family income with freelance articles, Sarah worked her way up to become editor-in-chief at a national children's magazine. Her e-mail asked me if I'd like to do another article for the publication.

For a moment, I considered what that meant. I was able to get background information on Devils Tower by writing a story on the country's first national park. Would the same work with Bear Butte? Maybe. Maybe not. Either way, it surely couldn't hurt anything.

I sent Sarah a reply, asking what type of story she was looking for. Her e-mail hadn't mentioned any specific subject matter, but rather "any interesting, historical places out in the wild, wild west." If I did it right, Bear Butte could certainly qualify.

And a story about the Butte would give me an excuse to go out there and ask questions.

Chapter Six

As far as I could tell, researching Bear Butte hadn't gotten me anywhere so I decided to try another tactic. I would look into the history of the Black Hills Motorcycle Classic. Maybe the link was there. Logically, the connection was probably with the victim, but I still didn't know who he was so that was a proverbial dead end. Until I could get a name to research—or anything else from the spirit world—the motorcycle classic was the only clue I had.

I looked at my watch. 10:15 a.m. It was supposed to be hot again, but a quick glance at the outdoor thermometer said it was barely eighty degrees. Much cooler then the triple digits of the past week. I could be in the middle of the Black Hills Motorcycle Classic by 11:30. Having successfully avoided the crowds there so far, I didn't know what to expect. Well, I'd heard rumors and I'd seen the news reports with the number of crimes committed thus far during the festivities. The driving under the influence and drunk and disorderly charges were one thing. The additional indecent exposure and public nuisance citations, on the other hand, made my head spin.

I didn't really want to take the kids with me, so I arranged for Meghan and Bobbi to babysit again. Within minutes I was out the door and on the road.

Motorcycles were more predominate the closer I got to the small South Dakota town where the classic was held. I parked at a church not far from Main Street, which had been closed to all non-motorcycle traffic for the week.

As soon as I got out of the car, my cell phone rang. This time I looked at the number before answering. Good thing, too, since it was my favorite FBI agent. Again.

"Are you busy?" He sounded as if he were talking with an old friend.

I wasn't expecting such a warm welcome from Joe. This new, more pleasant Joe Oliver was going to take some getting used to. Instead of saying this aloud, though, I just replied, "Um, not really." I felt like I was yelling in the phone since there were so many loud bikes driving past.

An unfamiliar noise came from my phone. It took me a minute to realize Joe was laughing. "You're wandering around at the classic, aren't you?"

I admitted I was and he admitted he was also. We made plans to meet a few minutes later at one of the food venders just off the main drag.

It didn't take long to find where we were to meet. I ordered a cheeseburger and a frozen lemonade. It was pure luck that there were few customers at this particular stand and I was able to find a picnic table situated off to the side where no one could eavesdrop. Moments later Joe, having traded his FBI-style dark suit for a pair of jeans and a biker t-shirt, joined me with a burger and drink of his own. His steel-grey eyes, which I knew from experience missed nothing, were hidden by a pair of mirrored aviator sunglasses.

"I thought you might show up here sometime," he said.

I didn't know how to respond to that, so I stayed quiet.

Joe must have taken my silence for guilt, because he continued. "I don't blame you. I didn't have much other information to share. But I have a little more now."

"You do?"

He nodded. "We got an ID on the victim: Robert Mesmer, 37. He was an insurance agent in Washington State. It looks like he came out for the Classic. We found a reservation for him at the Mato Paha Campground, but it was only made a few days ago. He had a wife of seven years, Ellen, and a three-year-old son, but neither of them came to South Dakota with him."

"Oh no." I felt a huge wave of remorse knowing that a young boy was going to grow up without a father.

Joe was quiet for a moment, sipping his own drink, before continuing. When he did speak again, I thought I detected a hint of remorse in his voice. "For the past twenty years or so, Mesmer hasn't had so much as a parking ticket."

"Then why would someone want to kill him? Do you think it was an accident?" I hoped that was the case, because that meant no one had purposefully made a young boy fatherless. Suddenly, my cheeseburger lost its appeal.

"That's where things get fuzzy," Joe replied. "While there was nothing for the past twenty years, there seems to be a whole lot before that."

I did some quick mental math. "But that would make him a minor, wouldn't it?"

Joe nodded.

A group of young men walked past, halting any further conversation between Joe and me. Loud and boisterous, they looked to be in their late teens or early twenties and were dressed accordingly with brand names embossed on their shirts and ball caps. As a group, they were paying more attention to the bikes and women then to where they were walking which brought them quite close to our table. Joe didn't speak until they were well out of ear shot. "But there was still a lot to be found."

"How? I thought records were usually sealed for juveniles. At least they are on all the cop shows."

Joe shook his head and I saw his left eyebrow peek over the top of his mirrored sunglasses. "You can't believe everything you see on television, Cerri."

"Oh," I replied, feeling thoroughly chastised.

My face must have betrayed my thoughts because Joe quickly spoke again. "But you're right. His juvenile record is sealed. Mostly. We ran his fingerprints through AFIS—the Automated Fingerprint Identification System—and got a hit on a cold case in Louisiana from twenty-one years ago. I called down there and spoke to the desk sergeant and he gave me the name of the detective who worked that case. The sergeant was a young guy, but he said the original detective on the case hadn't retired yet." Joe tilted his wrist a little leading me to believe he was checking the time on his wristwatch before continuing. "In fact, the original detective—a guy by the name of Rich McShane—is here. He's one of the cops that was involved with the altercation that lead to us finding Mesmer."

"Really? How weird is that?"

Joe shrugged. "It's the classic. There are more tourists in this

28

town this week then the official population. A lot of those biker tourists are cops. Some vacationing, some undercover."

His words put the influx of people into a whole new light.

"Anyway, McShane is assigned to some task force. He's supposed to meet us here in a few minutes."

I took a bite of my cheeseburger and wondered why Joe even needed me here if there were so many actual law enforcement professionals at his disposal. There wasn't much time to mull it over however, because we were soon joined by an older man who had the look of a life-long mechanic. Rich McShane looked to be in his late fifties. His salt-and-paprika hair had probably once been at least as red as my own and the stubble on his face still sported more red than grey. His eyes, also blocked by sunglasses, remained a mystery to me.

"Hey, hoss, how's it going?" McShane's voice carried a slight southern drawl.

He sat next to me and Joe made the formal introductions.

"You wanna know about Mesmer, right?"

Joe and I both nodded, but only Joe spoke. "Anything you can remember. Like I told you when we spoke on the phone, your sergeant in Shreveport could only give me so much from the cold case file. However, he said you had a phenomenal memory and you might be able to give us something more."

McShane shrugged and his cheeks turned slightly pink. "I don't know about phenomenal, but, yeah. I remember the case you're talking about and I remember Mesmer."

"You do?" I couldn't remember what I'd had for breakfast, so the idea that a police officer could remember details from a twenty-year-old case amazed me.

"Yep. He was a punk." McShane had spoken softly, but with authority. "He grew up in the Shreveport area, if I remember right. Very stereotypical background, he was raised by a single mother who worked as a waitress at some all-night dive. I'm pretty sure Mesmer had himself some gang ties. We'd picked him up for some small-time stuff—misdemeanor theft, vandalism, criminal mischief, minor in possession, that sort of thing. The makings of a criminal, for sure."

"I know the type," Joe interjected.

"Yeah, man, I bet you do. You see it same as I do."

Both law men nodded silently probably lost in their respective memories of "kids gone bad."

Joe finally broke the silence. "What about the cold case? Your sergeant said something about a botched burglary."

McShane grunted and clasped his hands together atop the picnic table. "Yeah, that. It was." He addressed his next comment to me. "I'm sure your partner told you—"

I opened my mouth to explain that I wasn't Joe's partner and only helping because I couldn't say no, when Joe interrupted. "No. I didn't tell her anything. I thought it would be best to hear from you."

"Alright then. Understand that it's been a few years and I'm not as young as I once was." McShane chuckled at his own admission. "But here's what I remember. And," he turned his full attention to Joe, "if I get some of the details wrong from whatever you know, feel free to correct me."

Joe nodded once.

"Anyway, as best as I can remember, there'd been some gang-type turf fighting going on between two wannabe gangs."

"Wannabe gangs?" I asked.

The Louisiana officer squinted and I wondered if I'd given myself away.

"Yeah, you know the kind," he continued. "Not the real badasses of the day, but the ones who thought they were. Punk kids who thought a gang sounded like a good idea and had started down the path to the state penitentiary. Anyway, these two gangs were both well known in the area for auto theft, drug trafficking. That sort of thing. And their territories had started to overlap. Neither gang wanted to back down or show any weakness."

McShane glanced around before continuing. "So one night, one group of punks broke into a mechanic shop run by the other group. Sorry, I don't remember what the punks called themselves, since they didn't last too long and I wasn't on a gang taskforce or anything then. Honestly, the name the punks used made no difference to me then and doesn't much matter now. And that mechanic shop was tore down and a strip mall took its place."

"Not important, I'm sure," Joe reassured.

"It was late. However, the gang who ran the shop, had recently stolen a car. From what I remember two guys were in the shop, basically cannibalizing the car for parts when Mesmer and his idiot friends showed up. By the time they left, there was one shot dead and another who ended up in a coma. He still can't remember anything of that night, so he was no help then. Now he's serving twenty-five to life at The Farm, so I guess he didn't learn his lesson, either."

"The Farm?" I asked.

"Louisiana State Penitentiary," Joe explained as McShane nodded.

The Louisiana detective continued. "Anyway, we never caught the shooter, but had some leads. That's where your guy comes in."

My sense of justice kicked in and I began to wonder if Robert Mesmer didn't do something to facilitate his death. A wave of guilt rushed over me at the thought, but my heart went out to the families of the original victims. "He was there? You can prove that?"

McShane shrugged. "He was there. I know it. Can't prove it, but I know it."

Afraid I would ask another question that would cast suspicion on my lack of law enforcement experience, I remained quiet. Joe, however, asked the question that had been on my mind.

"How do you know if you can't prove it?"

McShane shrugged again, tilting his head slightly to the left. "It's all circumstantial. And I could never put him in the building. There was a cigarette butt in the gutter outside with his fingerprints. According to the city contractors, a street sweeper had passed through the area about 45 minutes earlier, so the butt probably got there when the break-in happened. Unfortunately, we could never prove that."

Joe's nod, accompanied with the frown he now wore, spoke volumes. "Understood."

The two men sat in silence while a group of teenagers sauntered by. When they passed, it was Joe who spoke first, but his voice was quiet, barely above a whisper and I had to lean over the table to hear.

"Lieutenant McShane, I know it's been a long time and you're account is very similar to what your sergeant told me. However, would you happen to remember anything else about this guy? About Mesmer?"

McShane shook his head. "Not really. I guess the only thing that stands out is that I was always surprised he didn't end up like the rest of his so-called friends. They all ended up dead or at The Farm. He never really fit in with them, either. He was more...I dunno...respectful, maybe. The typical good kid corrupted by the wrong crowd. Part of me thought he mighta had a conscious about that night and been fed to the gators for it."

I gasped before I could stop myself.

"It was a possibility. I guess I'm glad he didn't seein's how he seemed to stay outta trouble ever since, but I wish he would have gained a conscious. I don't like having a cold case out there."

The two men continued talking in hushed tones while I tried to process the information they'd shared. Even with a name and a few details of the victim's past, nothing that I had learned so far would help determine who'd murdered the man.

At least not without some kind of divine intervention.

And that kind of help didn't seem to be showing up anytime soon.

The men's voices returned to their previous levels, not loud enough to be overheard by passersby but enough to turn my attention back to them. When I did focus my attention on the two law enforcement officers, they were both looking at me as if expecting something.

"Sorry, I was lost in thought." I was sure my face looked guilty since I wasn't paying attention to them, but at least I was being honest.

The Louisiana detective's brows creased just a little before he spoke. "I asked if there was anything else about that cold case you needed to know."

"Oh, um, no, I don't think so," I replied, feeling my face flush. "You've been very helpful." I hoped my voice sounded more confident then I felt.

McShane rose, extending his hand to first Joe than me. "Well, I hope it's helped." He turned his attention to Joe. "You'll call if you need something else."

"Will do. Thanks," the FBI agent replied. "And enjoy the classic."

"It's…interesting," the Louisiana lawman replied, a smile creeping over his lips as his head turned slightly toward the rumble coming from the nearby street. I followed what I assumed was his gaze to find a woman driving her motorcycle down Main Street. That alone wouldn't have been a sight, but the woman was hollering to attract attention and her clothing options made sure to keep the attention of every male around. Her neon pink bikini top covered just enough to ensure she didn't get an indecent exposure ticket and the matching motorcycle chaps made it hard for me to look away. The "girl power" part of my brain applauded her for wearing such an ensemble without a supermodel's body. The "overprotective mother" part of my brain was grateful Zach wasn't with me since I wasn't ready to answer questions about her exposed skin. I alternately felt embarrassed for her and wondered if she remembered to put on sun screen. There were places exposed on her that I wasn't sure had seen the sun since she was in diapers. I lowered my eyes to my long forgotten cheeseburger, although it wasn't easy to do. The woman was making such a spectacle of herself that it was like watching a bad car accident. You just couldn't help yourself.

While I'd been focused on the sight cruising Main Street, Lieutenant McShane had disappeared into the crowd. Joe waited until I turned my attention to him before speaking.

"You know, none of that was really public knowledge, right?"

His meaning was loud and clear—nothing I'd heard from the lieutenant was to be repeated. Ever.

"What changed him? Mesmer, I mean."

Joe shrugged. "After his move to Washington at age 18, there doesn't seem to be anything more on his record. He got a job, took the classes to become an insurance agent, kept his certification up, paid his taxes on time."

Joe and I sat in silence, each sipping our cool drinks, lost in our own thoughts.

I broke the stillness. "Could this have been revenge for the case the lieutenant was talking about?"

"Could be. I can't see much in his current life that would lead to murder, but we haven't explored all the options."

"All the options? Like a bad insurance settlement or something?"

"Or his wife having an affair. Or he had some type of argument with a co-worker. Or, hell, I don't know. It's all speculation at this point."

"Do you think his wife was having an affair?"

"She didn't come here with him," Joe answered. "Does that mean she was? Not necessarily. Maybe the classic isn't her type of thing."

A couple walked past us as Joe spoke. The man's neon green mohawk stood more than eight inches from his otherwise bald scalp. He led his companion by a dog collar that she wore around her neck, and her hair was streaked the same shade of green.

"Well, I can certainly appreciate that." At that moment, I didn't see the appeal of the classic, either.

Joe chuckled again. I noticed he hadn't removed his sunglasses, making it difficult for me to tell where he was looking. It was also disturbing to see myself reflected in the mirrored lenses, so it kept me from looking at the FBI agent for too long.

"We have someone in Washington interviewing her, and also Mesmer's co-workers." Joe didn't waste much time getting back to business. "I don't know if anything will come of those interviews, but my gut is telling me that this didn't have much to do with his life out there."

"Why not?"

"If Mesmer was killed because of something that happened within the past twenty years, why kill him here?" Joe's voice had resumed the ultra-professional tone I was more accustomed to. "It would be more logical to take care of business there. Not wait for him to come out here."

"Unless the killer wanted to throw suspicion elsewhere," I suggested. Maybe I'd read one too many mystery novels, but it seemed like a reasonable assumption. Then again, there was that cliché about assuming.

"It's a possibility. Like I said, at this point everything is a possibility."

"Besides, why would someone want to kill him over something that happened years ago?"

"Crime of opportunity? I don't know." Joe paused.

Another motorcycle roared down Main Street, the driver revving the engine and making conversation difficult. I looked up, watching the bike as it made it's slow crawl for all to see. Bear Butte loomed in the distance like some kind of guardian or defender or protector.

Protector? That reminded me of something. "What do you know about the Protectors of the Black Hills?"

Joe's brow furrowed. "I know they are dedicated to preserving the Black Hills. They aren't eco-terrorists, more like activists."

My eyebrow raised. "Eco-terrorists?"

"Yeah, they're more vocal, not violent. Why?"

"I found a web site when I was searching Bear Butte. They want to keep it as a sacred site. There was something about a lawsuit, but I didn't look too deep into that. I guess I was just wondering if maybe Mesmer was in the wrong place at the wrong time. But if they aren't a violent group. . . ."

"Like I said, everything's a possibility. But, you're right. They aren't violent. I guess it's an angle, though. I just don't see them as being involved at all. If they were trying to make a statement, chances are good the body wouldn't be hidden. Plus, we don't have any evidence that Mesmer was involved in anything environmental. Not even a fishing license."

After a few minutes of compatible silence, Joe spoke again. "I don't know if any of that will help you...."

I wasn't sure either, and told him as much. "But, you're right. It's a place to start."

He nodded before rising from the table. "I'll let you know when I find out more about Mesmer's life."

"Thanks. Maybe I can...find out something else."

"And, Cerri, thanks for agreeing to help," Joe said. "I really appreciate it."

35

With that, Joe turned and melted into the crowd.

I remained at the table, taking in the atmosphere surrounding me. Bear Butte sat, still keeping watch in the distance.

Suddenly, the cheeseburger, which I'd barely touched, lost its remaining appeal. I tossed it in the trash before heading into the crowd myself.

Chapter Seven

The drive home was far less congested because there were fewer motorcycles heading east. Few of the tourists were ready to return to their homes just yet. Back on the interstate, I managed to ignore the radio, lost in my own thoughts. Located only a few miles down the road, the Black Hills National Cemetery forced me back to the present. There's something about all those pure white crosses standing sentry in perfect rows that makes my heart swell with patriotic pride. Maybe it's because I grew up an Army brat, moving from place to place every few years as Dad climbed the ranks to general and these cemeteries were small plots of American soil no matter what country we lived in. Maybe it's because I grew up realizing that each cross stood as a silent witness over someone who sacrificed for my personal freedoms. Or maybe I'm just strange.

Whatever the reason, I couldn't ignore the feeling of needing to see those markers up close and personal.

I took the next exit and found a parking spot near the visitor's center. The moment I stepped out of the car, I felt the familiar mixture of calm and sorrow I've always associated with cemeteries. Even as a young girl, cemeteries didn't give me the creeps. Sure, I felt more somber in one, but never afraid. Often, there was a feeling of relief and love associated with them. Relief that suffering had finally ended and a sense of the love the living still held for those who'd gone before.

Funeral homes, on the other hand, were permeated with feelings of sadness and pain.

The visitor's center at the Black Hills National Cemetery was small yet efficient. A whiteboard announced that there were no burials scheduled for the day and, like so much else in the Hills this week, welcomed bikers to the classic. A touch-screen monitor served to help family members locate their loved ones' final resting places and also gave a brief history of the cemetery.

Since I didn't have a specific grave to visit—or even a name to search for—I didn't play around on the system for long. Within fifteen minutes, I'd given up the building's comfortable air conditioning for the stifling heat of the outdoors.

Because of the way the road wound its way through the cemetery, I couldn't drive straight out. The road continued on to a large gazebo-type building where services could be held. The best and most logical spot to turn around was the cul-de-sac in front of that building.

I made it to the turn-around when I noticed him off in the distance. He Who Waits was intensely studying a grave marker. It was like seeing a long-lost, yet completely unexpected, friend at a doctor's office in another city. I was both glad to see him, yet worried about why he was there.

I knew I needed to find out what he was staring at.

Taking a side road, I found a place to park close to where He Who Waits was standing. I got out of the car and headed toward the marble markers the shaman was scrutinizing. The look on his face didn't invite conversation, so I remained quiet waiting for the spirit guide to speak first.

"All cultures honor their dead."

We had been silent for so long and He Who Waits spoke so softly that I wasn't sure he had spoken at all.

"All cultures honor their dead," he repeated.

That comment didn't require a response, so I said nothing.

"When a Lakota dies," began He Who Waits, "his spirit lives on. The spirit is always present—even after the bundle is burned."

"The bundle is burned? What does that mean?"

"In Lakota culture, after a death some of the dead's possessions are placed in a bundle, similar to the prayer bundles you have seen."

I remembered the brightly colored sachets tied to trees I'd seen at Devils Tower. When I nodded my understanding, He Who Waits continued.

"After the time of mourning, the bundle is burned. Just because the bundle is gone, does not mean the spirit is. The spirit is always present."

"I'm not sure how this will help find the murderer."

"You must understand the culture. If you do not, you will not find the answers you seek."

"But Mesmer wasn't Lakota."

He Who Waits nodded. "You are correct. He was not. But he did have a culture. To find your answers, you must understand his culture."

"His culture?"

Silence again. I was about to repeat my question when the roar of motorcycles from the interstate reached us. I looked up to see a group of riders traveling west, presumably headed to the classic.

"His culture," came the steady voice of He Who Waits, "might not be where you first look."

I felt my brow wrinkle as I tried to understand what the shaman meant.

"Many years ago, children were forced to leave their homes and attend school far away." Sadness had crept into his voice. "They were expected to forget their language and customs. It was a difficult time for our people."

"The kids were sent to government boarding schools, right? Weren't they even discouraged from practicing their religion?"

"Yes, *Cuwitku*. And some children never found their way back to their homes. Our way of life was almost lost. Those children, however, were still Lakota. They had Lakota blood in their veins. Some were taught the old ways in secret. That is how our culture survived. Not all people can be so fortunate."

Realization dawned on me. "So the culture I should focus on is the one from his childhood? The one he gave up?"

I saw my companion nod once as he faded away.

As I headed back to the car, I called Joe to tell him to look closer into Robert Mesmer's childhood. I only hoped I wasn't leading him on a wild goose chase.

Chapter Eight

There was a lull in the dinner conversation. I couldn't bring myself to mention my meeting with Joe in front of the kids and frankly that's what was forefront on my mind.

As I glanced around the table, to see how close to finished each of the kids was, I noticed Zach's "I have something important to say" face.

"What's up, Zach?" I asked. I could hear him kicking the chair as he chose his words carefully.

"Have you noticed all the cool motorcycles, Mom? They're pretty much everywhere."

"Yep," I agreed. "And some of them do look pretty cool."

I could see the twins rolling their eyes, as if to remind me that the influx of motorcycles was also loud and annoying. Zach continued before either girl could voice an opinion.

"I wish I was old enough for one..." His voice was soft, but wistful.

Before I could inform my son that there was no way his eight-year-old self was going to get on one of those death traps, my best friend and the love of my life betrayed me.

"Ya know, there are motocross bikes for kids about your age," Matt interjected.

As I looked from my husband to my son, I noticed the glance they shared. Then it hit me. I was being set up. Those two had formed a conspiracy.

"No." I had visions of serious accidents. Not the "He Who Waits type" visions, but rather the "let's not have anything happen to my child" type. "You're too young and you could fall off and break your arm. Besides, you don't even know how to ride a motorcycle."

"I could learn," Zach announced with all the determination of an eight-year-old who wants something.

"I can teach him," Matt said at the same time. "It's like riding a bicycle."

Clearly the plot had been hatched during some clandestine father-son, male bonding moment. Yes, it was a conspiracy and yes, they had won. I looked from my husband to my son. "Okay. Fine. But if you break your neck, don't come crying to me." My stern words were negated by my resolute tone.

Zach pumped his fist and screamed "Yes." while the twins started laughing. All three children had huge grins on their faces and I knew I'd lost more than a battle over a motorbike.

I looked into the faces of each of my children. "Spill it. What's going on?"

Kenzie was the first to crack. "Daddy said that if Zach got a motorcycle—"

"We get a puppy!" finished Maddie.

"A what?" I asked, looking directly at my husband the conspirator.

The sheepish expression on Matt's face reminded me of his son. "Well, um, we have the room for one." He shot a glance at the girls. "I told them I'd talk it over with you."

There were a lot of things I wanted to say at that moment but, mindful that the children were sitting there, settled for "Really?"

Matt opened his mouth to defend his part of the plot he'd obviously worked out with all three kids, when the phone rang.

Normally, a ringing telephone would have been ignored during dinner.

Since this wasn't a normal dinner, I opted to answer the phone while Matt gave the kids permission to leave the table and go play. I could hear Zach dreaming aloud about the type of motorbike he'd soon have and the girls discussing dog names. I didn't check caller ID before I answered, even though I normally do. If I had, I probably wouldn't have answered.

"Cerridwen, lass, how is everything there?" My mother's Irish lilt traveled the phone lines, while inwardly I groaned. Mother had a way of calling when I least wanted to speak with her. This was one of those times.

Rather than tell her I didn't want to talk, I replied "Fine, Ma, how's everything there?"

"Don't give me that. I can tell you're upset."

Not only had I lost the battle over the motocross bike, I knew this battle wasn't going to end in my favor either. Battles with Mother never did. "I was just talking with Matt and the kids," I told her.

Mother's soft groan told me that she didn't really believe me however, she didn't pursue the issue. Her willingness to let my little white lie slide indicated she had something more important on her mind. Or else I was getting better at deceiving her and I didn't believe that for a single minute. In typical "Mother" fashion, she continued. "But something else is going on. I know it is."

Mother always knew things. Or at least she claimed to. My family tree was highly matriarchal. Mother called our ancestors "wise women," and all those women had…talents that didn't always conform to society's expectations. I rarely saw the wisdom in non-conformity.

Not knowing exactly how to answer Mother, I replied, "Let's just say it's been an interesting day, Ma."

Another dismissive sigh indicated she still didn't believe my half-truth. "If you don't want to tell me, that's fine."

Great. A guilt trip.

As Zach would have said, I folded like a rug. I started to fill her in on the events of the past few days.

When I finished, Mother remained silent, an unusual occurrence. When she finally spoke, she was full of advice. "Have you thought of contacting the spirits? Not your spirit guide, per se, but rather the wee spirits? The fairies?"

Fairies? I was just starting to wrap my head around the existence of ghosts and spirit guides and now she wanted me to ask Tinkerbell for advice? "No, I hadn't thought of fairies…."

Mother's third sigh annoyed me more than I thought possible, but she spoke before I had the chance to voice my frustration. "Of course you hadn't, Cerridwen. But you know the Sidhe will help if you ask them correctly."

While she was speaking, I sat back down at the kitchen table and rubbed my temples. Mother believed in these possibilities, but, despite having been raised on such stories, I had trouble accepting things I couldn't touch. I wracked my brain to remember anything I had heard about the Sidhe.

What I could recall wasn't encouraging. Most people thought of fairies as cute little creatures who enjoyed playing harmless pranks. I'd been taught that fairies, just like people, had their own personalities. Some liked tricks, some enjoyed housework, some gardened. Others were just plain mean. Mother had even taught us that the word *fairy* was similar to *human*; it was a generic word that had nothing to do with the culture or ethnicity of the specific creature. A year ago, I would have assumed those statements were only things of legend and part of the folklore Mother took as gospel. Now I wasn't as convinced.

I must have been too silent for too long, because Mother continued, her voice now full of reproach. "Hmmph. You've probably forgotten how to do that as well."

Mother could be awfully snarky when she wanted to be. It was even worse when she was completely correct.

Luckily, I didn't need to respond, since she continued without giving me a chance.

"Of course, it would be best if you had access to the trees," she said.

I rolled my eyes and rose to get a glass of water before sitting back down at the dining room table. At her mention of trees, I could feel a headache coming. I began to rub my temples. "Ma, we do have trees in South Dakota, you know. And the Black Hills National Forest isn't too far."

"But they aren't the same as back home," Mother replied. She had left Ireland at the ripe old age of eight, and although she had traveled the world with my father, Mother never referred to anywhere but Ireland as home.

"No. Most of the trees here are Black Hills Spruce and Ponderosa Pine, I think. Too bad those probably won't work." I tried to make my voice sound resigned. I started to stand, wanting to pace around the kitchen and in an effort to alleviate some of my nervous energy.

I didn't get far, though. Mother's words forced me to sit back down and reminded me of the headache I'd tried to forget. "Pines? Wonderful!"

"Wonderful?" I repeated, completely and totally lost. "Pine trees are wonderful?"

I could almost hear Mother rolling her eyes before she responded. "Pine trees are important, Cerridwen. They are the 'sweetest of the woods,' you know. They're one of the seven powerful trees."

"I thought all trees were powerful. Isn't that what you always taught us? To honor nature?"

"Cerridwen, lass, do you only listen to half of what I say?"

It didn't matter how old I got or how far away I lived, Mother had the power to make me feel like a disobedient child. Thankfully, I didn't need to respond since she continued.

"Of course all nature is sacred," she began. "But different parts have different purposes."

"Different parts?" I repeated.

"Different plants, different minerals, different animals—they all have different purposes in the grand scheme of the Universe."

Even though she couldn't see me, I nodded in agreement. Besides sounding vaguely familiar, her words made sense. Possibly because spiritualism was one of Mother's favorite topics, she didn't seem to notice my silence.

"Pine trees are best for purification or fertility." It was Mother's turn to pause. I could hear her clicking her tongue, a habit she had when deep in thought. "I'm sure, though, that the Dryads can be contacted anywhere...."

I started to ask her about Dryads. There was only so much I could remember about the various species of fairies. Especially when I hadn't thought them to be real. Before I could ask, however, Mother continued.

"Do either of the girls have the gift?"

Despite the fact we were talking about spiritual mumbo-jumbo, my first reaction was to remind Mother that the twins' birthday wasn't until May. As if she knew where my mind was, she didn't give me a chance to speak.

"I mean the gift of speaking to the fairies, of course."

"Honestly, Ma, I'm not sure. I wouldn't even know how to discuss that with the girls."

My statement was meant with another dismissive grunt. "No matter. If neither of the girls are attuned to the fairies, there are other ways to ask the wee ones for their help."

Knowing this was going to take a while, I searched for a pencil and paper to take notes. When it came to the spirit world, Mother knew what she was talking about. And it was a subject she could talk about for hours on end.

Chapter Nine

Mother and I had been on the phone for more than an hour when we finally said our good-byes. Matt had already put the kids to bed and hit the sack himself. As for me, my head was reeling from talking with Ma and I knew sleep would elude me for some time to come.

I made my way to the living room, hoping to engage in some mind-numbing activities while I processed the situation I found myself in.

Still amazed at the information Mother had given me on fairies, I didn't know if I should try to contact any or not. I briefly considered asking Matt for his opinion, but the thought sounded too strange to my own ears, let alone to say to my more scientific-minded husband.

There was nothing on television and no one to talk with, so I headed into my home office. For a moment, I toyed with the idea of checking my e-mails, but decided my thoughts were still too jumbled to do that. Instead I lit a white candle and asked really nicely for He Who Waits to show up.

"Um, hello," I started nervously. "He Who Waits? You around? Busy? Can we talk?"

There was no answer. I wasn't really expecting one. But I was hoping. I mean, it worked last time, so it could have worked this time too, right?

I kept asking for He Who Waits to show up until I felt like a complete idiot—which truly wasn't very long. The shaman didn't appear, nor did I expect him to. Disappointed, I blew the candle out and stood to leave, thinking I might as well try to get some sleep.

He Who Waits was standing in the doorway. "*Cuwitku*, you must be quiet in order to hear," he said. "Patience is a lesson you have yet to learn."

Patience had never been my forte. If I could spend time not waiting, I was all for that, but I knew that wasn't something I needed to explain to the shaman. Aloud I asked, "why so quiet?"

46

"To teach you to listen," was his reply.

I started to roll my eyes when he continued.

"You cannot listen while you are speaking. And you must listen to find the truth."

The reprimand struck home, but the grandfatherly figure in the doorway wasn't finished.

"There is an ancient saying, *Cuwitku*, that you have two ears but only one mouth. It is to remind us that we must listen twice as much as we speak."

I instinctively opened my mouth to protest before snapping it shut again. I knew he was right.

If my reaction surprised him, he didn't show it. "You are seeking direction?"

With his earlier reprimand still ringing in my ears, I only nodded.

"Then how may I help you?"

"I don't know," I answered honestly. "I'm not even sure where to start. I mean, you told me to start at the beginning, but what does that mean? The beginning of Bear Butte? Or the beginning of this man's life? Or some other beginning I haven't found yet?"

"We all have a past, *Cuwitku*. You were not always a wife and mother." By calling me *Cuwitku*, which I knew meant daughter, his point was effectively driven home.

"So this man—Robert—was killed because of something he did in his past?" An idea occurred to me. "Or maybe because of something he was?"

The spirit guide nodded and I opted to continue, trying for more information.

"But he isn't from here. How am I supposed to learn about his past?" I was genuinely confused. "At least last time you asked me to work with the FBI you gave me some information to go on."

He Who Waits was silent for a moment before pointing to the computer on my desk. "You use technology to find some answers, do you not?"

"Yes. There's tons of information on the Internet."

"Have you tried seeking answers there?"

Before I could stop myself, raised my eyebrows sarcastically and shot the spirit a look which said "you've got to be kidding me." Aloud I responded, "Do you have any idea how many millions of web sites are out there? People can post just about anything on the Internet."

"Some things are more reliable, are they not?"

"Well, of course." I wasn't sure what he was getting at, but I was glad to be on a tangent that might lead somewhere. If that somewhere was away from violence and murder, even better. "There are personal sites that aren't as reliable, but you can find just about any public record if you know where to look. And newspapers...and magazines...there's a lot of research type things available."

"Exactly," was all He Who Waits said.

I yawned, thinking that He Who Waits hadn't really helped. Nor had my mother. I now had some directions to head in, but they were at opposite ends: technology and fairies. How could two thing so different work to lead me to the correct answer?

As I reflected on my confusion I was reminded of the cartoon bear who often complained about his head full of stuffing. It could have been the late hour or the topic of conversation, but either way I felt lost.

"Your *wawanyake* will help you as you help him," He Who Waits said.

Telling me that "my policeman" would help didn't inspire confidence either. Last time we'd worked together my motivation was to stay out of jail. His was to put me there. Thankfully, we both lacked that particular chunk of motivation this time around.

The face of He Who Waits took on the look I'd come to associate with his explanations. "You each have strengths. You each have access to information the other does not. Only by working together will justice be found for Robert."

It was a variation on a speech I'd heard before, but nothing in his words helped me determine my next step. I didn't have a chance to ask the ancient shaman anything else, however, since he chose that moment to disappear from view.

Chapter Ten

The kids had a busy day planned. All were enrolled in an art class in downtown Rapid City and we tried to do all of our running around as long as we were right there. That meant a trip to the library and some grocery shopping. Throw in a picnic lunch at the park and some time to either run wild there or, if the temperature was warm enough, an hour or so at one of the city's outdoor pools and the Baker clan wouldn't be home for most of the day. Unfortunately, I now had to fit in finding a murderer in the day's already busy schedule.

And a nap would be much appreciated since I didn't get much sleep the night before.

As Matt ate his breakfast, I asked about his plans for the day. Admittedly, however, I wasn't paying much attention, since I was trying to figure out how I was going to get the kids to their art class and still have time to do some sleuthing. He must have noticed my lack of attention, despite the grunts and nods I interjected to the mostly-one-sided conversation.

Finally, he touched my arm and asked, "You haven't heard a word I've said, have you?"

"Um...no. Sorry. I'm just a little preoccupied."

"Yeah, I could tell." Matt sat his coffee mug down. "Wanna talk about it?"

I grimaced. "Not really. I'm not sure you could help. I mean, I know you want to, but this is a ... thing."

Matt nodded. I always expected him to be more skeptical then I was since he didn't grow up with the same beliefs I had, but it never worked out that way. As a scientist, Matt spent his days analyzing rocks and teaching college students to do the same. He liked to be able to see and feel things, so his acceptance of other-worldly matters always boggled my mind.

Matt was done with his breakfast so I took his dishes and put them in the sink. "I kinda need to run some errands today, but the kids have art."

"No problem. I'll take the kids, just tell me what time to have them wherever." Matt gave me a shy smirk. "Besides, I told the kids we could go look at puppies today."

"Puppies. Great." I looked Matt in the eyes. "Do we really need a dog?"

"Well, I did promise the girls...."

"Because you told Zach he could get a motorbike." I was still frustrated, but at least now I was frustrated about real-world situations instead of hocus-pocus stuff.

Matt shrugged, looking like a little boy who got caught with his hand in the cookie jar.

I didn't want to fight with Matt over something as silly as a puppy and I knew my mood could easily lead to an argument. Instead of pursuing our current line of conversation, I asked, "Are you sure you can take the time off today? It really would be a big help."

"No problem. I don't have classes today, and I can run over to the college and get some work done while they kids are at art. It will be fine. We're between semesters anyway."

Since that was settled, I made sure Matt knew when and where to take the kids and decided I would head back to the classic. I hoped to be able to find more information about the man who had been killed at Bear Butte. I still wasn't positive *how* I would get any information, but I knew I needed to do something.

Zach was still asleep as I got ready to leave, but I heard voices coming from the girls' room and knew they were awake. By the time I'd showered and gotten dressed, however, even Zach was out of bed.

"I'm getting a motorcycle," came my son's sing-song voice from the living room.

His boasting was met with an answering, "We're getting a puppy," from the girls.

It was time for me to go.

As I grabbed my purse and headed for the door, I suddenly remembered the conversation with my mother. Fairies.

Instead of heading out the door, I turned around and headed for my office. Somewhere in there was the book I needed. I never got rid of books.

After twenty minutes of searching, I finally found what I was looking for. Years ago Mother had sent me a book about fairies. I hadn't read the book, but I remembered receiving it. It was still in one of the boxes I hadn't bothered to unpack after our move the previous year.

I spent another ten minutes skimming the book before I found what I knew would be in it – a concoction said to call the fairy folk.

Grabbing the book, I once again headed for the door. I would need to stop at the mall and pick up a few items. Then I'd go into the hills near the Black Hills Motorcycle Classic and see if my plan worked.

It couldn't hurt. I mean, how could calling the fairies be wrong?

Chapter Eleven

I made a quick stop at Rapid City's mall before heading west on the interstate. At the Black Hills National Cemetery exit, I decided to put my plan in action. The cemetery was on the south side of the interstate, but there was a camp ground surrounded by trees to the north. I figured I could find the perfect spot.

The Alkali Creek area was owned by the Bureau of Land Management. Trees and a self-guided nature trail were located next to a small camping area more suited to afternoons out then long term stays. There weren't even shower facilities. But the area was perfect for what I intended to do.

The parking lot wasn't too full despite the proximity to the Classic, but I could see evidence of campers in the area. There were tents and confirmation of recent fires around the campground and some sites had clothing hanging from make-shift lines.

I found a parking spot and loaded my recent purchases into my purse. I got out of the car and headed toward the trailhead. I mentally inventoried what I had brought with me when I remembered one more item I needed. I went back to the car and got a pink satin ribbon Kenzie had left in the backseat last week.

After putting the ribbon into my pocket, I again headed toward the trailhead. I took one of the maps from the self-serve pamphlet stand and started walking.

I followed the trail past some picnic tables and over the creek. By keeping an eye on the map and an ear out for other hikers, I left the trail near what I guessed to be the half-way mark. I couldn't hear the creek anymore and I was starting to get a little nervous. What if someone saw me? What if it didn't work?

I shrugged a little and shook my head. Negative thoughts weren't going to help me. A year ago there was no way I would have been on this mission, and now I was trying to psych myself up for it. The irony wasn't lost on me.

Forging my own path, I headed east, away from the parking lot.

Being directionally challenged, I didn't want to go too far, but I needed privacy. Or at least I thought I did. Either way, being seen wasn't high on my list of priorities.

After a few minutes, I found the perfect spot. A large pine tree stood slightly apart from other trees. Feeling a bit like a fugitive, I looked around to see if anyone was paying attention to me.

I found a spot at the base of the tree and sat down. I took a deep breath to calm my nerves before rummaging through my purse for the items I'd brought with me. Even though I knew I wasn't doing anything wrong, I felt a little like a fugitive.

"Face it, Cerri, you just aren't cut out for a life of crime," I said aloud for no other reason than to hear my own voice. "You aren't even cut out for a life of sneakiness."

I made myself comfortable on the forest floor and opened the book I'd brought with me. It took a few minutes, but I finally found the page I was looking for.

Placing the book on the ground next to me, I used my wallet to keep it open to the right page. I placed Kenzie's pink ribbon next to the book. Then I took the items I'd purchased at the Mall – a small tube of glitter and a prism – and laid them beside the ribbon.

My heart pounded in my chest, but I wasn't sure why. I knew I wasn't doing anything wrong, just different than what most adults would do.

How many adults went tramping through the forest in an effort to talk to fairies?

I took a few more deep breaths to calm my nerves. Logically, I didn't understand why I was so uneasy but the butterflies in my stomach were hard to ignore. In the distance, I heard a woman calling for a child to slow down. Her words may have inspired the child to slow, but they made me want to hurry.

Deciding I better get started, I said a silent prayer and stood up. Memories of my childhood came flooding back as I cleared my mind and my space for the task at hand. Facing north, I took one step forward and called to the elements—just like my mother had taught me when I was young. Amazed that I remembered what to do, I repeated the process while facing east, south, and west.

When that task was finished, I stood back in the center of the circle I had just created. If I had been apprehensive about someone catching me calling the elements, I was downright nervous about my next step.

I opened my mouth to speak and found myself at a complete loss for words. Remembering back to my childhood, I was sure Mother always made some type of a rhyme, but I had never been good a thinking up words to rhyme. At least not on the spot. The stubborn perfectionist in me won out and I tried anyway. "I really hope my voice will carry," I whispered, "to a helpful, little fairy. There is something I need to know. If you help me now, then I'll go."

Nothing happened.

I waited for what seemed like hours, but was probably only a few minutes. Patience had never been among my strengths. I could hear the woman calling to the child again, only this time from a point past me on the trail.

I was just about to give up when the memory of my own mother's voice came flooding back to me. *You must always be extra polite when asking for help, Cerridwen,* I remembered her saying.

"Please," I begged.

I had barely gotten the word out when pastel balls of light began to float down in front of me. They looked like colorful snowflakes falling from the treetops. The sight was mesmerizing. It was so beautiful that I almost didn't notice the buzzing noise the balls of light were making. The noise got louder and louder until I realized it wasn't a buzzing, but talking.

The balls of light were talking.

"Whatcha want?" The voice was childlike. I couldn't tell if it was a boy voice or a girl one. Heck, I couldn't even tell which little ball of light was speaking to me. The entire effect was rather disconcerting, sort of like how I imagined Sleeping Beauty must have felt after a hundred years of sleep.

The amazement must have been evident on my face, because one ball of light stopped six inches from my nose. As I watched, the pink ball elongated and began to morph into a girl. Her hair was short, dark and slightly spiky, her facial features were delicate, without the chubbiness that I associated with children. Her pink gossamer wings glittered in the sunlight, contrasting nicely with her purple skirt and white top. Her tiny, bare feet tapped impatiently in the air as she spoke. "Hey! I'm talking to you! You called us. Now, whatcha want?"

At least now I knew where the voice was coming from, but the rational part of my brain still had trouble processing the experience. The sensible part of my mind had always considered this a fool's errand. That part was now eating crow.

Finding my voice, I replied, "I really need some help."

The pink girl still floating in front of me put her hands on her hips the same way my girls did when they were particularly annoyed. "Yeah. We got that part. What do you need help with?"

"I need some information and I know you guys see everything." I didn't really know if fairies saw everything, but it was worth a shot. "I'm trying to find out information about someone—a person—who died. Well, was killed, actually."

Talking about murder felt strange considering the beings surrounding me looked younger than my kids. Even though the fairy floating in front of my nose had probably been alive longer than my own mother, part of me felt like I was ruining her innocence by discussing the horrors of humanity. Her reaction to my statement was to shrug her tiny shoulders, roll her eyes and ask, "So?"

I wasn't prepared for such a response. "What do you mean, so?"

"I mean, so. Who cares? That's the humans' problem. Why should we be concerned?"

"Why shouldn't you? You should help me because it's the right thing to do." I knew it wasn't a great reason, but it was the one I came up with. It was easier to argue with my kids since I could always say "because I'm the mom" to them. For a brief moment I wondered if this was how He Who Waits felt when I challenged him. Probably. Returning my attention to the Sidhe I asked, "Don't you want to help people?"

"Not usually," came the fairy's reply.

That just blew my mind. It may have been naive, but I was under the impression that the fairies would want to help. "What do you mean, 'not usually?' Someone was killed and you could help. Isn't that enough?"

While I'd been speaking to one specific fairy, the others had morphed from their balls of light into tiny, translucent beings—each of them looking like young children. From somewhere on my right, came a chuckle. On my left, I heard some grumbling and one pretty adamant "no way." Asking the fairies for help seemed to be a waste of time and I was getting ready to apologize for bothering them when I heard, "Come on, Vesta. It might be fun."

Those seven words worked better than someone screaming "Silence!" would have.

I quickly glanced around, trying to determine who spoke. Since every little face was staring at a point behind me, I assumed that's where the speaker was. While I debated turning around to thank my ally, the fairy I'd been speaking with flew past me with a speed and agility that would have made a race-car driver envious. I turned at a more reasonable pace.

The pink fairy girl was nose to nose with another fairy; this one a green male. Or at least I assumed it was a male, since this fairy wasn't wearing a skirt and the hair was in a short buzz cut.

As I watched the two of them in some silent power struggle, I wondered how much more surreal my afternoon could get. Part of me wanted to wake up from the obviously odd dream I was having and another part wanted to tell the two fairies to behave themselves. My frustration got the better of me.

"Grow up," I said aloud.

All eyes turned to me once again and, with them, a bad case of nerves.

"Excuse me?" the pink girl demanded. "What right do you have in telling us anything?"

If I had to pick one of my strongest assets, diplomacy would not be one of them. I took a deep breath and decided to give it a try anyway. "It's Vesta, right?"

She nodded curtly.

"Okay, Vesta, I don't. I don't have any right to tell you what to do. I came here to ask for your help, that's all. And I understand the

56

desire to not get involved with other people's problems. I would really prefer to mind my own business, as well."

There were a lot of head nods and sympathetic sounds in response. Even Vesta seemed to lighten up as I spoke, her shoulders relaxing and her stance becoming more relaxed.

I continued my soliloquy. "Look, I know most humans don't believe you even exist. And we've messed up a lot of things we know *do* exist." I waved my hands indicating the trees surrounding us. "We should do a whole lot better at taking care of the environment and solving our problems and getting along with each other. But we don't. At least for now."

I paused, not knowing exactly what to say next. Too afraid of losing their attention, or my nerve, I didn't stop long before I continued my ramblings. "And we may never get it right. We're humans. We mess stuff up. But you guys, you're better than humans. You're magical in ways we could never be. You know things we can never know."

This bit of my impromptu speech was met with another round of agreement from the fairies surrounding me. Before I could continue, however, the fairy who interrupted me earlier asked, "If you don't have faith in humanity, why should we help you?"

It was a good question. "It isn't that I don't have faith in humanity. I just know we don't have all the answers. As for why I need your help, well, that's a little more complicated. Mostly, I need your help because I don't know where else to turn."

"What type of help do you need?" the green fairy asked.

"I'm trying to find out what happened to a man who was killed. I don't know why he was killed or much about his life. I'm just. . .well. . .no one deserves to be murdered, do they?"

Vesta spoke. "No, but I'm not sure how that becomes our problem. We didn't kill the guy."

I took another deep breath. "No, you didn't. And it's not your problem, either. But I don't know where else to turn." Instantly, my mother's stories came back to me and I remembered her telling me that the Sidhe often liked to have their ego's stroked. It was a tactic I decided to use. "I know fairies are smart and knowledgable and you know things humans don't. I was hoping you would be willing to help me."

That tactic must have worked.

"We are very knowledgeable," agreed Vesta. "If we help you—and that's a big if—what would we get in return?"

Mother had warned me about that, too. The fae rarely did anything for nothing.

"I, I don't know. What would you like as payment?"

Then I witnessed the second fairy disagreement of the day. Vesta announced she wanted a favor. The green male demanded pizza. This disagreement was one I thought I could end quickly.

The favor I had expected. The pizza was easy. "You'll have both," I said. "In fact, I'll throw in this ribbon and glitter, too."

A round of cheering followed, convincing me I'd done the right thing. Mother was right: the fae were fickle beings.

I just didn't know how fickle.

Chapter Twelve

The more I spoke with the troop of fairies who had answered my call, the more they reminded me of immature children. Vesta seemed to be their leader, but the fairy who had challenged her—I learned his name was Bill—had his own following. The whole thing reminded me of *Lord of the Flies*, and I just hoped I wasn't going to be a casualty in their power struggle.

Bill's group wanted pizza. They probably would have taken chips and chocolate if I'd offered it. They seemed to be ruled by food.

Vesta's followers wanted the glitzy, sparkly things. That group's actions reminded me more of the cartoon fairies which permeated American culture.

Both groups, however, decided I owed them a favor for their help.

I had a feeling that being in debt to one group of fairies was going to be bad. Being in debt to two separate groups was going to get me in trouble. Probably a lot of trouble.

Unfortunately, I didn't see any way around it.

After reluctantly agreeing to their terms, I told the fae what little I knew about the murder. "Do you know anything else? Can you tell me who did this?"

Vesta rolled her eyes. "Humans," she mumbled. "They expect all the answers at once."

Bill stifled a chuckle.

"Okay, so you don't know. What *can* you tell me? It looks like this guy was only here for the Black Hills Motorcycle Classic. Whoever killed him is probably here for the Classic, too." I wasn't sure how accurate that statement was, but it seemed logical. Quickly, I scanned the faces of the winged creatures surrounding me for some sort of confirmation, but they gave me none. There was no sign I was wrong, though, either. Without some type of validation either way, I just kept going. "I mean, that only stands to reason, right? If Robert wasn't from around here, his killer probably wasn't either. I hope there are some answers for his family. His poor son is going to grow up without a father. . ."

"What do you mean 'his poor son'?" asked Vesta.

"He had a child?" Bill demanded simultaneously.

The concern I heard in their voices came as a surprise. Nothing up to this point had implied the fairies thought of anything beyond themselves. "Yes, he had a son. Why? What difference does that make?"

Vesta opened and shut her mouth a few times, squinting at me with such fierceness that her eyebrows not only seemed to meet above her nose, but almost overlap each other. Had she been one of the green-skinned fae she would have looked exactly like a fish out of water.

Bill's response was more subtle. "Children are innocent."

Ignoring Vesta, I asked, "Are you more willing to help because a child has been left fatherless?"

"Yes." Bill sighed like an old man. "Children are helpless. We— the fae race, I mean—vowed long ago to protect the innocent. Animals, plants, children; they are all innocent. It's adult humans who are the cruel ones."

Remembering my teenage years, I considered arguing with him but thought better of it. Thinking of my own three children, however, I could see his point. "So because the man had a child, you'll help me. Even though the child isn't around here and probably isn't in any danger?"

Vesta turned to Bill. "I think she's finally got it."

Her eye roll was almost audible. I opened my mouth to scold her when the high-pitched buzzing I'd heard earlier resumed. This time it was obvious that the fairies were speaking to each other in their native tongue. Even though I couldn't understand a word being said, I got the message loud and clear. Bill and Vesta were having a fight. Or at least a heated discussion.

First Bill was sweeping his arms and pointing while Vesta shook her head. Then the roles changed and Vesta's tiny fingers jabbed at the air while Bill's arms remained firmly crossed. At one point they were even nose to nose, both screaming and waving their hands. Eventually the two appeared to strike a compromise, the muscles in their shoulders started to relax and their voices grew calmer. Both fairies turned to their respective followers and spoke.

Even though they had apparently stopped arguing, neither Bill nor Vesta looked at me.

Finally, I couldn't take it anymore. "Excuse me? I'm still here, you know."

Bill nodded as Vesta snapped, "We know." She seemed less snarky than she had been. Or else I was getting used to her attitude. Either way was a step in the right direction. I hoped.

As I pondered this change in attitude, many of the fairies began to shimmer and squish back into the balls of light I'd first seen. A handful of the creatures had even managed to float away before I found my voice. "Where are they going?"

"Half of them are going west toward Washington to learn what they can about the family," Bill explained. "The rest of us are going to stay around here to see what we can find out."

His words shocked me. Sure the fairies had agreed to help, but I hadn't expected . . . . I didn't know what I actually expected.

My amazement must have been evident because Bill flew a few inches closer, his tiny head tilted to one side giving him an even more compassionate air. "We will help," he stressed.

Relief flooded over me at his assurance. At least until Vesta spoke.

"But we aren't doing it all."

"I would never expect you to," I replied, upset that she would think I wanted them to do all the work. I spent the next few minutes explaining my relationship with Special Agent Joe Oliver and why he had asked for my help.

The fairies asked far fewer questions than I would have if the situation had been reversed.

When I felt we'd covered everything important that I knew, I tried again to get some information from the fae. "Isn't there anything you can tell me now that might help? I mean, I know you've just learned about this, but maybe . . . ." I indicated toward the other fairies, or rather to the absence of so many of them. Presumably, they had taken off to begin their respective assignments. For all I knew, the fairies could zap themselves back and forth through time and space and communicate via telepathy. "Can you at least point me in the right direction?"

There was only the distant rumble of motorcycles as Bill and Vesta exchanged a knowing look.

I may not know the language of fairies, but I could decipher that expression. It said, "Do we tell her or not?"

I gave the two another moment to decide before asking, "What? What is it that you know?"

Their silence remained unbroken. I wasn't sure which was more annoying, the quiet or the chatter. Either way my frustration was reaching the point normally reserved for the hours before a major deadline when I hadn't even started writing the copy for the story. I didn't need a mirror to confirm that my facial features were taking on what Matt called my "stressed out mom face." It must have worked on the tiny beings surrounding me, because Vesta finally spoke up. "I don't know nothing. But he does."

Bill blushed. Or at least I assumed the dark green overlay he had acquired was the equivalent of a fairy blush.

I turned the power of my "mom face" fully to Bill. "Spill it."

"I don't know much," he began. "Not really. I don't know anything about the dead man at all." For the first time, Bill's voice had taken on a whinny quality reminding me of Zach when he was extra tired.

Bill's voice may have been whinny, but I was the one suddenly feeling extra tired. I wanted to tell the fairy to quit whining and ask him what the heck he did know, but I didn't want to cause a scene—or worse, offend the entire Sidhe race.

I must have exuded some type of annoyance, because I didn't have to wait long for Bill to continue.

"But I might know something about who did it."

This was more than I could hope for and my annoyance quickly changed to anticipation. "You do? Tell me what you know. Please."

Bill shrugged as if my begging didn't matter to him one way or the other. His shrug carried my frustration back like a wave to the shore. I was about to say something—though I hadn't really thought anything through—when Bill spoke.

"Don't get too excited," he said as a lop-sided grin spread across his face. "What I have to tell you may not be that helpful."

"I'll be the judge of that." As soon as the words were out of my mouth, the image of a badly acted TV detective show flashed into my mind. With any luck the fairies had never seen such a show. Considering the relationship between Bill and Vesta, maybe they preferred courtroom dramas or tabloid-style talk shows. Just thinking of the tiny fae tossing chairs at each other in front of a live studio audience brought a smile to my face.

"If you're done smirking, maybe we can get on with this." Vesta's snarky attitude returned with a vengeance.

Bill and I both ignored her.

"Anyway," the male fairy started. "All I know is there are tribal marks on him."

"Tribal marks? On him? Like tattoos? So a man killed Robert, right?" This was the first clue they'd given me. It was the first clue I even had. The only clue I was able to share with Joe, although there was no way I would tell him how I got the information. If I couldn't mention He Who Waits, there was no way I could bring myself to discuss the possibility of fairies. He would have me locked in the loony bin for that.

"Yes. A male. With tribal marks."

"So, a man with tattoos," I repeated. "Wait. Do you know how many men have tattoos around here? Especially during the classic? What kind of tattoos?"

Now it was Vesta's turn to smirk.

Ignoring her again, I continued. "Tattoos are so common now. And there are tattoo artists who make the Black Hills Motorcycle Classic their vacation. They even set up shops during the Classic just to meet the demand."

Bill only shrugged.

I let out a frustrated sigh. "Okay, so can you tell me what the tattoo—the tribal mark—looks like?" I had visions of the traditional tribal arm band tattoos that seemed to be so popular if the media was to be believed. Maybe a band of black ink that would be easily covered by a T-shirt making finding the mark even more difficult. This sounded like the proverbial needle in the haystack.

"The mark is a tribute to the ancestors," said Bill. "The type that honors the dead."

"Honors the dead? Like a tombstone? Not an intricate design in a band?"

Vesta rolled her eyes while Bill shook his head.

"Honors the dead, but not like those." He pointed to the Black Hills National Cemetery. "And not a band of knotwork."

"Okay, not a tombstone. A name?"

The fairies remained silent.

I kept wracking my brain for other symbols of ancestors or ways to honor the dead and came up empty. "Isn't there anything else you can tell me?"

"Humans always expect all the answers at once." Vesta repeated her earlier comment.

"All I can tell you is that the marks are the same as those which honor the ancestors." Bill's voice took on a quality that reminded me of Matt patiently explaining the virtues of metamorphic rocks. Again.

Obviously I wasn't going to get much more out of either of the tiny winged creatures. I took yet another deep breath so that my voice would be free of sarcasm before speaking. "Okay, so we're looking for a man with a tattoo that honors the dead. I really appreciate the help."

"You should," came Vesta's reply.

"Believe me. I do."

While we'd been talking, the remaining fae had departed leaving only Vesta and Bill below the tree with me. The air began to twinkle a little as the last two fairies prepared to leave without another word.

"Wait." The echo surprised me and I quickly lowered my voice. "How will I find you again? I mean, what if I learn something important? Or if you do? How will we find each other to share information?"

I sort of expected Vesta to reply with "don't call us, we'll call you," which brought to mind an image of the tiny creatures on miniature cell phones. Instead it was Bill who answered.

"We'll find you."

One thing I did not want was the possibility of having to explain talking fairies—or talking to myself—to my kids. They didn't need to think their mother was crazy. As I started to share that concern, however, the fairies vanished leaving me alone except for two small rabbits.

One's fur had a slight pink undertone. The other had deep green eyes.

Chapter Thirteen

I wasn't any closer to learning anything useful about the dead man. I wondered if my mother's advice had been worth following or if she'd sent me on a wild goose chase. By the time I came to the conclusion that it didn't matter, I was only a few blocks from the town's Main Street, which was closed to everything except motorcycles. Fighting traffic for a parking spot large enough for my vehicle didn't sound like fun, so I turned into the parking lot of a church. They advertised "All Day Parking" and even as cheap as I was, it was easier to pay the five bucks then to find another spot. I might be frugal, but I didn't think there would be any free parking for something larger than a motorcycle in the entire town.

Besides, the walk wouldn't kill me.

As I paid the attendant, my eye was drawn to one of the many buttons pinned upon his vest. The words "Black Hills Motorcycle Classic" surrounded a skull. Not the bone white skull with a menacing grin surrounded by flames I would have associated with bikers, but a black skull covered with lime green swirls and dots on a vibrant red background. The pin was both eye-catching and mesmerizing.

The attendant caught me studying the pin, and gave me a quizzical look. "Something wrong?"

"No. No, everything's fine," I blurted embarrassingly. "I was just noticing that pin. The one with the skull."

The attendant's face relaxed, apparently deciding I wasn't a complete creep for staring. "Interesting, isn't it? Some guy was handing them out earlier. He had a ton of them."

Speechless, I only nodded. Something about that pin danced around the edges of my memory like the chorus of a Broadway musical: you knew it was there, but it was still enough in the dark that trying to make out exact moves was impossible. I could only hope my mental spotlight would eventually move so I could see what was teasing me.

"Do you know what they mean? The pins, I mean." I felt like I was babbling.

The attendant shrugged. "Advertising something, I'm sure, but I don't remember what."

After thanking the attendant for his time, I headed toward the epicenter of the rumble. Even from blocks away, the roar of thousands of motorcycles was overpowering.

I walked the two blocks to Main Street before I realized I didn't have a plan. Not even a bad one.

I kept walking, turning left with the crowd when I reached Main Street. I spent so much time trying to avoid running into people that I'd completely abandoned trying to devise any plan other than not being trampled in the crowd. Of course, that meant I wasn't paying any attention to where I was walking, either.

I probably wouldn't have walked into anyone, though, if I hadn't been roughly pushed.

"Hey, watch it!" The woman was tall and thin, almost willowy. Dressed in a pair of denim cut offs, a flowery tank top and flip flops, she was dressed more conservatively than most twenty-something women at the rally. Her short, dark hair looked easy to manage and was surrounded in a wrath of white daisies, reminding me of a 1960s "flower child." At her feet sat a large, white bucket filled with flowers of various species and colors.

She had been talking to another young woman, a few inches shorter with long blond hair gathered in a French braid. The second woman, also with a large white bucket, rolled her eyes before picking up the bucket and mingling into the crowd.

"I'm so sorry." I took a step backwards, bumping into someone else who responded with a curse. Ignoring them, I turned my attention to the young woman I'd first jostled. "Completely my fault. I think I was pushed, but I wasn't watching where I was going anyway."

"Really?" She was mildly sarcastic, but I had almost stepped on her.

"I'm very sorry." I certainly hadn't meant to run into the poor girl, literally or figuratively.

She sighed impatiently. "It's okay. No biggie."

I'm not sure what came over me, but I knew I had to talk to her. "Let me buy you something to drink…a soda or some lemonade? You know, to make it up to you."

The woman grabbed her cell phone out of her back pocket, checked the time on it, and shrugged her shoulders. "Sure. I'm due for a break and business is kinda slow." She picked up the bucket and carried it as easily as if it were an empty grocery bag.

I followed her toward a group of picnic tables tucked between two buildings. If nothing else, the Motorcycle Classic was a lesson in using space.

"They have the best lemonade here," my companion stated matter-of-factly. Since almost every lemonade stand boasted the same claim, I opted to take her word for it.

Taking the heat into consideration, I quickly ordered two of their largest size and brought them back to where the woman was sitting at a picnic table which had seen better days. I only hoped few splinters would fester their way out of the dry, abused wood while we sat. I lowered myself onto the bench opposite my companion, determined to sit in exactly the right spot on the first try. There was no way I wanted to be wiggling around now, or pulling splinters out of body parts later.

The younger woman seemed oblivious to the neglected wood. In fact, she seemed bored. Until I noted that her eyes didn't miss much. She may have practiced keeping her face expressionless, but her eyes reveled that she missed very little happening around her.

"Here you go," I said, handing her one of the cups which was already covered in condensation from the melting ice. "Again, I'm really sorry for bumping into you. I wasn't paying attention."

"Happens a lot around here," she replied. "Not many people offer to buy a lemonade to make up for it, though." Her eyes narrowed just a little as she spoke, her distrust evident in her tone.

There was no way to answer that, so I remained content to sip my own drink. After a bit of silence, I spoke again. "My name's Cerri. How long have you been selling flowers?"

"A while. It's a fun way to see the bikes. I'm Judy, by the way."

I wasn't sure where to take the conversation. I needed to find information about Robert, but I didn't know if Judy even knew the guy. How exactly does a person even go about finding that out? This was nothing at all like writing an article for a magazine. There I at least had the illusion I was speaking with someone who knew something. Rather than risk sounding like an idiot by asking about dead men, I said "I'll bet it is. Probably see all kinds of interesting things."

Judy laughed, the accompanying smile lighting up her face. That was how she should always look, I thought.

"Interesting doesn't even begin to cover it," she said. "Plus, I like camping. I get to spend the week up here and have the flowers delivered each day. Sure beats me having to fight the traffic from Rapid."

"Camping? You mean you stay up here for the week? Even though you live less than an hour down the road?"

Judy nodded. "The shop sends flowers up every day, and I make sure to start selling early. If I need more, I call down and they have more sent up. In exchange I get to stay out here for the week. It's kinda like a working vacation."

I nodded as an idea was forming in my mind. "Where do you stay?"

"There's a campground not far from Bear Butte, out on Highway 34," she said. "My parents make sure to rent a cabin every year. It's a place to deliver the flowers without fighting all the traffic. Plus it's nicer than staying in a tent."

"Do many locals stay there?" From the talk I'd heard most locals waned to the leave the area when the motorcycles arrived. I hadn't heard of any wanting to spend more time surrounded by the influx of tourists.

"Nah. Maybe some of the beer girls, but not even many of them?"

"Beer girls?" That was a phrase I had never heard.

"Yeah, you know, the girls who come up just to serve beer at one of the beer tents? Lots of times they're the party girls who'd be here anyway. At least the ones I know," she explained. "Plus, they work much different hours than I do."

"Why do you do it? Wouldn't it be more comfortable to sleep in your own bed?" As soon as I asked the question, I realized how old I must sound to the young woman.

Judy sipped her lemonade again. "Truthfully? It's fun. I live at home summers while I'm going to college. This is an adventure. I know my parents worry about me, but it's only a week and it helps them out, too. They own the flower shop, you know?"

We slipped back into a comfortable silence. I thought about what she had said, turning the information over in my mind. In the street, I could see a biker slowly cruising Main Street. A large flag fluttered in his wake.

"Wait a minute. Where did you say you're staying?"

"Out by Bear Butte. At the Mato Paha Campground. It's usually a pretty quiet place, as far as the rally goes."

"Mato Paha? Why does that sound familiar?"

He Who Waits appeared behind the woman. "Because it is where Robert vacationed."

Judy, who didn't hear the shaman speak, shrugged as she took another sip of her lemonade. "It's not a real creative name. I think it's Lakota for 'Bear Butte' or something. There were a ton of cops out there the other night."

I went out on a limb, hoping she knew something that could be helpful. "Did you hear about the guy who was killed? I think he was camping there."

"Yes! He had been staying like three spots down from me!" It was slightly macabre, but there was excitement in Judy's voice.

"So you knew him?"

She shrugged the way teens and young adults have perfected. "Not really. I mean, I'd seen him sitting outside his tent and checking his bike. But he was really quiet, especially by Classic standards. Didn't really party, kept to himself. Honestly, when I saw him around, I thought he looked kinda sad. I'm pretty sure I never even spoke to him."

Disappointment set in, but I tried not to let it show.

"My friend might have, though," she continued.

70

Sleeping Bear

"What?"

"You didn't think I stayed out here alone, did you?" The expression that crossed Judy's face could only be called a snicker. "Brittany and I have been working the classic for three years. It's the only way my parents would let me stay out here."

"So your friend might have talked with him? Brittany?"

Judy's brow wrinkled a little as she thought back. "Sort of. I mean, she did, but not really."

Now it was my turn to wrinkle my brow.

"Brittany was kinda flirting with some other guy. Well, instead of just telling Britt he wasn't interested, the guy starts being a real as…um, jerk. Yelling and screaming. It was like he flipped out or something. Really weird."

I nodded, encouraging her to continue.

"Anyway, the dead guy—I don't know his name—he comes over and tells Britt to go back to our campsite. Then he tells the other guy to knock it off. He was really calm, but sorta scary at the same time. He reminded me of that saying, you know, the calm before the storm."

"And you didn't know either one of those guys?"

Judy shook her head.

"Do you know anything about either of the guys? Do you know where either one was from? Did they come to the classic together? Anyone who might have had a problem with the guy who was killed?"

I must have asked too many questions or acted too strangely because Judy's face closed back up. No longer open and welcoming, she once again wore the mask of teenage indifference. "You a cop or something?"

I thought about saying, "Not a cop, just someone who talks to ghosts and spirits and the cops would like me to help figure out why the guy died," but I knew that sounded ridiculous. Even at the Black Hills Motorcycle Classic where just about anything was fair game. Aloud I gave a noncommittal, "something like that."

She pulled out her cell phone again, checking the time. "I need to get back to work. Give me your digits. If I think of something, I'll text you."

71

I rattled off my cell phone number as she plugged it into her phone. "If you think of anything," I started, "anything at all...no matter how odd...I'd really appreciate it."

She shrugged once again. "Yeah. No prob." Grabbing her bucket of flowers and her half-finished lemonade, Judy disappeared into the crowd.

As I sat at the table, I figured I would never hear from the young florist again.

I was wrong.

Chapter Fourteen

I watched Judy disappear into the crowd. I didn't think she'd actually call me. I wouldn't call some crazy lady who basically bugged me while I was working. Even if the crazy lady did buy me lemonade. At least I had something I could pass on to the FBI.

But a man with a tattoo? How much help would that actually be?

My lemonade was almost finished and all the ice had melted. The splintered seat at the table was not getting any more comfortable. One of the young women working at the lemonade stand kept looking my way, as if I was taking up valuable retail space, although there wasn't a line of people waiting to sit on the arid, splinter-ridden bench.

Standing up, I tried to nonchalantly check for splinters attached to the fabric of my shorts. Since nonchalant has never been one listed among my virtues, to spectators I probably looked like I was adjusting my undergarments. With that realization, I could feel my cheeks begin to flush and knew it had nothing to do with the heat. Being easily embarrassed was something I'd never managed to outgrow.

I grabbed my purse and what was left of my lemonade before turning to leave.

Despite my emotional discomfort, I decided to stick around town for a bit longer. I'd fought the traffic into the normally quant town, so I might as well walk down the street. I could at least say I'd been there.

As I walked down Main Street, I was amazed at the sights. I hadn't bothered to really look at the bikes when I met with Joe the day before. Now that I took the time to appreciate them, I was stunned. There were bikes of all colors and sizes with decorations of every shape and size. There were bikes with traditional flame-type designs, bikes with side cars, and bikes made out of cars. Even though my knowledge of makes and models was limited, I could tell just about every manufacturer was represented.

The few blocks were an assault on the senses. Not only were the bikes colorful and loud, but the exhaust fumes mixed with the scent of various foods being sold in lean-to style tents. The sidewalks were so crowded with people it was hard to move without bumping into someone. Hawkers peddled their wares, which ranged from t-shirts and alligator tales to tattoos and body piercings. No one needed to leave town without a souvenir of some type.

A crowd gathered in front of one window, where a young man was getting what looked like his fourth or fifth tattoo, and that was how many I could count considering the current work of art was spread across his back and he was, therefore, facing away from the window. I didn't want to speculate about how much ink wasn't visible. The tattoo artist, a middle-age man covered in colorful ink, stopped his work long enough to wipe the design with a piece of gauze, cleaning the blood from the skin so he could continue to work. The design, which took up most of the younger man's back, caught my attention. Two combat boots propped a semi-automatic rifle straight up. Balanced upon the butt of the weapon, a Kevlar-style helmet rested, below the boots a name, rank, and dates were listed in flowing script.

I knew the design. I'd seen it gracing the walls of my parents' home growing up: a visible reminder of a deceased soldier.

An image honoring the dead.

I'd never been in a tattoo parlor before, and I wasn't sure I would ever get inked at a motorcycle rally, but I entered the shop anyway.

A steady buzzing assaulted my ears, reminding me of a swarm of cartoon bees.

"Ready for some ink?" A woman in her early 20s approached me. Her appearance reminded me I was out of my element. Her dark brown hair, streaked with turquoise, pink, and purple, was pulled into a messy bun. The colorful artwork gracing her arms and upper chest clashed for attention. Combined with the multiple piercings adorning her face, I assumed she either had a very high pain tolerance or actually enjoyed the pain she inflicted upon herself. I wondered what her parents must have thought of the image she portrayed.

When I didn't answer, the girl repeated her question.

"I'm sorry. I'm just looking." I wondered if people could actually look around at a tattoo shop, the same way they could at a department store.

The girl just shrugged and turned away, heading back to a counter I hadn't noticed before. I watched her go, trying not to stare. By averting my eyes, I noticed what looked like books of frames attached to the walls. They reminded me of the displays at the big chain stores where people could flip through to see which posters were for sale in the tubes below. Only instead of posters, each frame held dozens of tattoo designs.

I headed toward the nearest set, grateful to have some purpose for being there. A few of the employees and customers glanced my direction as I made my way toward the wall. But most ignored me as I did them.

I flipped through the designs, admiring some of the artwork. I hadn't realized how many different styles of tattoos where available and began to wonder if finding a tattooed man wasn't an even bigger challenge than I'd originally thought.

I'd made it through the first book of frames and had started a second when the same girl from earlier approached again. "Are you looking for something in particular?" This time when she spoke, I saw a glimmer of color in the mouth and wondered why anyone would pierce their tongue. Another reminder that this wasn't my normal world. Whatever that was.

"I'm looking for something to honor a person who died. Do you have anything like that?"

"We have lots of memorial flash."

"Flash?"

She nodded toward the frames I'd been looking at. "Generic art. You don't have any tattoos, do you?"

"That obvious?"

Her laugh was light and airy, putting me more at ease than her appearance had. "Don't sweat it. We get lots of newbies in during the classic." As she spoke, she walked toward another set of frames a little further down, motioning for me to follow.

"Do you know what type of design you want?" She flipped the

75

frames to the beginning and began pointing out various designs. "Or even where you want it?"

Afraid she might stop helping if I told her the real reason I was there, I answered, "Um, I hadn't given it much thought. Does it matter?"

"Tattoos are addicting. But they're also permanent. You want to make sure you get something you like in a place you want it. They are expensive pieces of art placed forever on your skin. You don't want to regret it later."

I found it ironic that she'd be giving me such a lecture, but nodded my agreement anyway.

"Who is the tattoo going to honor?"

I hadn't imagined she would ask that, so I said the name of the first person who came to mind. I followed with a silent prayer that my sister would forgive me.

She showed me a grouping of various angels and another of crosses, many could be personalized with names and dates.

Even though I didn't know what design I was looking for, I didn't think these were right. Logically, the fairies would have described angels or crosses in some other way. Not as a tribal mark honoring the ancestors. Of course, that assumed fairies used logic similar to mine, which was probably debatable.

As the young woman flipped a few more pages, she explained that any tattoo could be in honor of a someone, not just the crosses or angels. "Like that kid over there," she said, pointing to the young man being tattooed in the window. "He lost his best friend in Afghanistan, so he's getting a traditional military memorial design."

I nodded. "I noticed that. What about something tribal?"

She raised her eyebrow and offered another shrug as she flipped through some other pages. As she did, a design caught my eye.

"Wait a minute." I put my hand out to stop the metal frame from advancing. The page I'd seen was filled with colorful skulls similar to the one on the parking attendant's button. "What are these?"

"Those aren't really tribal," explained the young woman. "They're Mexican Day of the Dead skulls. The real skulls are usually made of sugar and can be left as a tribute to ancestors who have passed away."

Her recitation of the tradition stunned me. My silence earned me another shrug. "I'm a history major with a Spanish minor. I just work here as a receptionist."

"Do a lot of people get them as tattoos?"

"Some. They can be really colorful, as you can see." She pointed to the framed page where skulls were decorated with bright flowers and swirls, each individual in their designs. The young woman paused, studying the frames with a critical eye. "Ya know, some of those designs could be considered tribal, I suppose."

For the first time since Joe had asked for my help, I thought I might have something to give him.

The young woman didn't notice my silence. "We're getting a lot of requests for the skull designs. I'm not sure if it's just the in design, or if the custom motorcycle company has something to do with it."

"Custom motorcycles?"

"Yeah. Bone's Bikes. They use the Day of the Dead skulls as part of their logo. They're sponsoring a bunch of stuff here this year and really making a name for themselves. Some celebrity even ordered one of their bikes and a magazine had a huge write up about how great the work was. Got them a lot of publicity. I'm surprised you didn't hear about it."

"It sounds vaguely familiar."

She shrugged again. "Anyway, have you decided what kind of tattoo you want?"

Panic set in. Needles had never been my friends. "Um, no. I better think about it some more."

She nodded. "Good idea. Are you local?"

"Yes. I live near Rapid City." I wasn't sure what that had to do with anything.

"Great. I'll give you my card. When you decide, just call and make an appointment with anyone at Momma Bigg's."

Once again, I had no idea what she was talking about. The confusion must have been evident.

"Peggy Biggerstaff owns this place, Momma Bigg's Tattoos and Piercings."

"I didn't even notice the name when I walked in. Sorry."

"No worries. Momma Bigg's is open all year. Ask for Sarah when you call."

"You're Sarah?"

She nodded again. "Sarah Emily Parker. Not to be confused with the actress."

Smiling at her attempt at humor, I took the card she handed me. "Thanks for the help. I appreciate it more than you know."

Back on the crowded Main Street, I considered calling Joe with everything I'd learned. The background noise, however, hadn't dwindled as the day's temperature rose. If I wanted Joe to hear what I had to say—and to hear him in return—I needed somewhere more private. Unfortunately, my car was in the opposite direction from the direction the crowd was moving. Rather than fight the crowd, I opted to move with the flow of traffic, giving me the opportunity to peruse other vendors.

I had no intention of purchasing anything; I didn't need any more t-shirts and I had no need for any motorcycle accessories since I didn't even know how to ride one. Frankly, I couldn't always keep my balance on a bicycle. A motorcycle—both heavier and faster than a 10-speed—just seemed dangerous. And, therefore, much too risky for my son. I could feel my hair turn gray just thinking of it.

As I continued down the sidewalk, I tried to push any thoughts of danger out of my mind. Concentrating only on the moment, I wasn't really surprised when I started to notice the scent of worn leather. Between the chaps, the vests, and the jackets, entire herds of bovine had been slaughtered for the week's wardrobes. The only shocking part was that I hadn't noticed the scent much earlier. Especially since I had become used to the smell announcing the arrival of He Who Waits.

Despite the smell's logical explanation, I found myself searching for the elusive shaman. As I scanned the crowd, however, the scent vanished. Instead of finding He Who Waits among the crowd, my eyes landed upon a colorful skull decorating a long banner, which read "Bone's Bikes" in a skeleton typeface. The actual vendor's tent was hidden by the crowd of people, but I had no reason to head in that direction.

Almost as soon as I'd decided to pass the tent, another crowd of people appeared, slowing any progress forward or back. With the increased number of people, the leather-scented air seemed to close in on me. The overall effect made me uncomfortable. I had never suffered from demophobia, so I wasn't sure why the crowd seemed to bother me now. Taking some deep breaths, I kept moving, hoping that an opening would present itself and I could let the throng of people pass me by.

Just as I was starting to compare my situation with that of the lemmings forced off a cliff, I found my out. Without warning people began to veer off from the pack and I could move at my own pace without being forced to move with the crowd. Seizing the opportunity, I paused at the first vendor I could: Bone's Bikes.

Chapter Fifteen

Bone's Bikes was allotted more space than I'd originally thought. In addition to the deep red awning-style tent I'd seen from down the street, motorcycles were parked facing the area like spokes around a wheel. The perfect chrome finishes reflected the sunlight in ways that caused the bikes to glow. I was thankful I remembered my sunglasses.

I took a moment to admire the bikes while I tried to sort out why I felt led to the booth. Since moving to South Dakota, I'd come to realize there was no such thing as coincidence. It was a realization that would have made my mother proud if I were to ever admit it to her. Instead it made me nervous. Between the cryptic fairies, the distinctive button the parking attendant wore, and the colorful Sarah Emily Parker, there had to be something I was supposed to learn from this company in particular. Why else would the skull design keep coming up?

"I'll bet you're in the market for a two-fifty." The voice was deep, yet smooth, like bitter dark chocolate and was accompanied by a touch on my upper arm.

I turned as I spoke, finding myself face to face with a biker. The man before me had dark, penetrating eyes and olive skin. His bald head had clearly been shaved, rather than a product of genetics. His tattoos were more faded than the ones I'd watched being created at Momma Bigg's and at least one looked like it could have been an amateur job; it lacked the style and sophistication of the flash Sarah Emily had shown me. What really struck me, however, was the man's body shape: he reminded me of a bulldog, a broad, muscular upper body with thin, short legs. I might have laughed if he hadn't been sporting some frightening patches on his well-worn leather vest.

"You'd look great on a two-fifty. You don't look like the type of woman to be content to ride on the back," he said.

"Me? Oh, I don't ride," I confessed. "I don't even know how."

The man facing me chuckled. "You could learn. Must be

interested to be wandering around here."

I shrugged, not really knowing how to answer.

He must have taken my shrug as some type of agreement because he continued. "Thought so. Let me show you some bikes you might be interested in."

Finally finding my voice, I replied, "Actually, I'm interested in a motocross bike. For my son." I glanced at the vehicles surrounding the make-shift tent. "But you probably don't have anything that small."

He rolled his head to each side, as if trying to crack his neck. "Actually, all of our bikes are custom made. Motocross isn't a problem."

I didn't feel confident enough about the subjects of motocross or motorcycles to ask intelligent questions, but I could tell none of the bikes in my line of sight were small enough for my son to ride and said as much.

"I only have the bigger bikes here. I didn't think there would be much demand for the smaller bikes during the classic." He paused, motioning for me to stay put, before reaching toward the card table behind him. I hadn't noticed the piles of literature before. He handed me a glossy tri-fold brochure as he continued. "Take this. It has some starting prices, some design options, and my contact information. I'm Victor Helms, by the way. The phone is a cell. If you decide on something in the next week or so, I'll still be around."

I glanced at the brochure, noting the 504 area code. "You aren't local?"

He shook his head. "Nope. I'm only here for the classic. But I've got some custom upgrades to do and have some other business to take care of before I head back home."

"Okay, well, I'll take a look at this and see what I think," I said, even though I was sure Zach didn't need a motocross bike. And the girls didn't need a puppy. But I also knew the kids had joined forces with their dad and I was probably going to lose both battles.

Shoving the brochure into my purse, I turned to leave. Between the sun's rays and the reflection of heat from the parking lot, I longed for the air conditioning waiting for me in the car. Getting away from the crowds of the classic was going to be an added bonus.

The trek back to my vehicle seemed much less crowded than what I'd experienced earlier. I was even able to browse a few of the t-shirt vendors who set up shop along the way. Since it was so hot, taking the brief respites under the shaded awnings was a treat. I looked forward to the next vendor, just to get the sun's rays off my head, neck and arms. With my red hair and fair skin, there was no doubt in my mind that I was going to be the shade of a lobster by the time I was done.

Once I reached my car, I turned the air conditioner on full blast, content to let even the warm air blow on me just to feel the breeze. It wasn't optimal, but it felt much better than the heat outside.

Before I left the parking lot, I decided to call Joe and tell him what little I'd learned. Even though talking on the phone while driving wasn't illegal in South Dakota, I didn't want to take the risk with the increased traffic. Leaving my purse on the passenger seat of the car, I grabbed my cell phone and dialed the number I had for him.

Joe answered on the second ring. "Oliver," came his curt greeting.

"Agent Oliver, it's Cerri. Do you have a minute?"

Papers shuffled in the background as Joe replied, "Sure. Whatcha got?"

I explained to the FBI Agent that I took a trip to the classic and what I'd learned from Judy the flower merchant.

"So you just happened to bump into someone who could help? And then she decided to talk to you?" Joe sounded skeptical.

"I know it sounds fantastic," I said, remembering the sensation of being pushed. "I guess it was just luck."

"Luck. Right."

I ignored that. "Anyway, I got her contact info. And I know where she's staying. Maybe it would be worth talking to her. You, I mean, talking to her." Whether it was the heat or nerves, I rambled on, knowing I sounded like an idiot but not being able to stop.

"Give me what you've got on her."

I could hear scratching on the other end of the line as I gave Joe the information I had about Judy and her friend, Brittany.

After repeating everything back to me, Joe asked, "Did you. . .find anything else?"

What he really meant was *did a spirit tell you something else I should know?*

"No. I'm sorry, Joe, there's nothing else."

Joe started to talk when my purse hit the floorboard of the passenger's seat. Since I was still sitting in the parking lot, however, there was no logical explanation for the mess.

"Damn," I muttered, leaning over to throw everything back into the bag.

"What's wrong?" Concern crept into Joe's voice. "Are you okay?"

"Yeah, I'm fine." I grunted as I stretched to reach the receipts, pens, and other junk that had fallen out. "I dropped something. What where you saying?"

"I said that if you did find something more to let me know." He sounded guarded, as if he knew I wasn't being completely honest with him.

"I will," I said making another reach for escaped items from my purse. Mentally, I made a note to throw out a bunch of unneeded papers I seemed to be carrying around when I got home. Under my wallet and some loose change was the brochure I'd picked up at Bone's Bikes earlier. "Wait a second."

Joe didn't say anything. I could still here background noise, so I knew he was still on the line.

"I might have something for you to look into."

"Okay…"

"It's probably nothing." The idea of the decorated skull being important sounded a little crazy to me, so I could only imagine what it would sound like to someone who dealt in facts.

"Cerri, why don't you let me decide that?" Once again I had brought out annoyance in the FBI Agent's voice. I could picture his jaw starting to clinch as he began to reprimand me.

"This is going to sound weird," I started.

"Spit it out."

"Check out someone with a tattoo. A tattoo that honors someone else. Maybe someone dead."

"What?" That settled it. Agent Joe Oliver had reached a new level in annoyance. "Do you realize how many people in the general population have tattoos? Let alone in the Black Hills this time of year?"

"I know it's a needle in a haystack kind of thing. Believe me." The air conditioning had cooled the car down to a more comfortable level, so I turned the blower down to a mild breeze as opposed to the hurricane force I originally set it to. "And I stopped in at one of the tattoo places here. There are a lot of designs honoring the dead. Unfortunately, I can't even tell you which design to look for."

On the other end of the phone, Joe let out a defeated sigh, prompting me to offer an apology.

"Don't worry about it," Joe replied. "It was a long shot, anyway."

"I've got some . . . feelers out, so maybe I'll have something else in a day or two."

"I appreciate it. I really do," Joe began, "but we might be in a bit of a time crunch. Officially, the classic only lasts a week. Two if you count all the set up and tear down that the vendors do. If the person we're looking for is only here for the classic, we may not solve this."

No pressure there. "I understand. I promise, I'm working on it the best I can."

"Hey, Cerri, don't get me wrong. I do appreciate anything you can find. Really." His voice had lost its annoyance and now sounded more resigned, as if an unsolved murder could be a distinct possibility.

"We'll get whoever did this, Joe. I will do everything I can to help. Don't give up."

He chuckled. "No worries. Hey, hold on a second."

I heard him speaking to someone in the background. When he returned to the phone, he said, "Cerri, I need to let you go. The agents who talked to Robert's wife are on another line. I'll call you if I learn something useful."

As we said our good-byes and Joe reiterated his intention of calling back in a few hours. He thanked me again for agreeing to help. It sounded as if he was resigned to the fact that I wasn't going to be helpful in solving the case. Not for the first time, I wondered why He Who Waits bothered showing up at all if he wouldn't give me the information I needed to make a difference.

"Because alone you do not think you are capable," came the shaman's reply, startling me to the point I gasped.

I still hadn't disconnected the call with Joe, who heard my surprise. "Cerri? Is everything okay?"

"Yeah, I'm fine. Let me let you go. I'll call you if I learn anything else." I hung up before Joe had the opportunity to say anything else. Or to question me further.

Without saying another word, I pulled out of the parking lot and headed toward the interstate. The drive took much longer than usual because of the traffic and additional, temporary four-way stops the city put in place because of the increased population. It took more concentration than usual to fight my way out of the town. Once I hit the interstate, I broke my self-imposed silence.

"What was all that?" I knew He Who Waits was still around because I could smell the leather I pictured him wearing. It didn't matter how many times I'd seen him, I still had trouble convincing myself I wasn't imagining things.

"What was what, *Cuwitku*? You make little sense to me." He Who Waits sounded exasperated, a common situation when we talked.

I gripped the steering wheel just a little harder, trying to keep my temper under control. "Don't call me 'daughter' as if nothing happened. You threw my purse on the floor."

"You were forgetting an important part of what you had learned."

Had he been visible, I would have given him a dirty look rather than responding. However, it's difficult to know where to shoot such a look when the other participant in the conversation is invisible. Instead, I silently counted to ten, hoping that my own frustration would subside when I reached the double digits. It didn't. "I told him what the fairies said, which wasn't all that much, honestly."

"Many times those things which seem to be the the most insignificant are also the most important."

"That almost sounded like you were trying to help," I responded, slightly ashamed at the snarky tone I recognized in my own voice.

"Cerridwen, our goals are similar. We both desire to see justice accomplished." He Who Waits sounded offended.

I wasn't sure which was worse, the tone he had now or the one he used to reprimand me. "Look, I'm sorry. I'm just frustrated. There's so little time to figure this out. And I'm not sure I'm being much help to Agent Oliver."

"Many times those things which seem to be the the most insignificant are also the most important," the shaman repeated.

"You know that doesn't help, right?"

He chuckled, but didn't say anything.

I didn't get much further down the interstate when my cell phone rang. Without checking the caller ID, I answered, expecting Matt to be wondering where I was. "I'm on my way home, honey. I'm so sorry—"

"Cerri, this is Joe. Can you meet me at the Mato Paha Campground near Bear Butte? Something's come up and I think you'll be able to help."

"Me?"

"This is something that might require your special brand of help, if you know what I mean."

I agreed, despite the ominous tone of Joe's request.

I had no idea how ominous the meeting would turn out to be.

Chapter Sixteen

I took the next exit off the interstate and made my way to the campground, alone. I'm not sure when He Who Waits disappeared, I only knew he was no longer hanging around.

Once at the Mato Paha Campground, I had no trouble finding where Joe would be. The number of police cars at the entrance made for a logical place to search.

I parked the car, got out and headed toward the crowd of law enforcement officers and a few large, hyper dogs that looked like they wanted to attack. I didn't get far when I heard someone calling my name. Turning toward the sound, I saw Joe motioning for me to join him. A few of the bystanders looked questioningly at me as I headed in his direction, and their scrutiny made me ill at ease. Uncomfortable being the center of attention, I tried to ignore the stares and hurried to where Joe was in an animated conversation with a group of sketchy looking men. I would not have wanted to meet any of them in a dark alley and I was grateful in the knowledge that Joe was one of the good guys. I could only hope that he was going to break from the pack, tell me whatever was so important and let me head back home quickly. Glancing at the sky, I could see storm clouds start to roll in. The temperature began to drop and I wondered how bad the upcoming storm was going to be. In addition to beautiful landscapes, South Dakota offered a wide variety of weather—sometimes changing in just a few hours.

Standing at the outskirts of the group near Joe, I watched a man being put into the backseat of an SUV similar to one I'd seen Joe use when on official FBI business. A large man, he was a generous mix of muscle and fat. His hair was just below his collar and looked as if it hadn't been washed in a month. A leather vest covered his heavily tattooed chest. From where I stood, it looked as if the ink spread to his arms and neck. As a uniformed police officer roughly guided the man into the car, the biker shouted profanities aimed at the crowd, slurring his words as he did so.

As I watched the scene unfold, I heard the unmistakable tone of He Who Waits, who had obviously not left, only disappeared from view. "Things are rarely what they seem."

Before I could formulate any type of answer, Joe was standing beside me. I hadn't noticed him approaching. He gently grabbed my elbow and turned me toward the police car where the drunken biker was now throwing a fit in the backseat.

"I need you to talk to this guy," Joe explained, indicating to the police car.

My eyes widened as I realized what he was asking. "Him? In the back? You've got to be kidding me."

Joe ignored my surprise. "It'll be okay. The guy—he says his name is Karl McMillian—saw our dead guy having an argument. It's probably the same argument your flower seller saw, but I can't be sure."

I remained silent, waiting for Joe to tell me he was only kidding and I wasn't going to have to talk to a man who embodied every negative biker stereotype I'd ever heard, though nothing in our history had indicated the FBI agent had much of a sense of humor. When I found my voice, I asked, "What did he do?"

"I'm fairly sure he just witnessed it. I'm not sure he did more than that."

"No. Just now. Why is he under arrest?" I hoped the man in the backseat wasn't the murderer, though he looked perfectly capable of it.

"Drug bust."

Great. I had to go talk to a man on drugs. My own string of profanities echoed through my mind before I once again heard the voice of He Who Waits. "Things are rarely what they seem, *Cuwitku.*"

Before I could say anything, Joe continued, his voice barely above a whisper. "Karl's a good guy. Don't worry." Louder he said, "When I heard the location, I decided to head here myself. That's when I thought you might be some help."

By this time, we'd reached the SUV and Joe opened the passenger's side front door. "Karl, chill out and tell her what you saw." To me, Joe said, "Do me a favor and drive down the road before you start talking to him. There's a park a few miles from here that will work."

Now I had to go somewhere alone with a drugged out, crazy man?

For the third time, He Who Waits stated, "Things are rarely what they seem."

Karl responded with another string of slurred profanities and I again regretted ever agreeing to help Joe.

The FBI agent shook his head as he motioned for me to get into the car. "I'll meet you there in a few minutes. With your car."

I silently pleaded with him not to leave as I got into the SUV. When it was obvious that Joe was leaving me with the man, I forced myself to take a few deep breaths and willed my heart to stop its jackhammer-like thumping in my chest. From the time I pulled the large vehicle away from the campground until I found the park Joe had mentioned, I whispered "this is just another interview" and "the place is crawling with police, so I'll be fine" over and over. The words didn't stop the fear gripping my chest, but it did sound a little reassuring. I parked and, after adjusting my body so I could see the man in the backseat, said, "You saw a fight the other day, right?"

Karl, his ice-blue eyes full of distrust and contempt, glanced around. It looked like he was trying to make sure he wasn't overheard. When he spoke, his voice was kind and clear. "What all did he tell you?"

That wasn't what I'd expected him to say and the words—combined with the gentle tone—took me by surprise. "Excuse me?"

"Joe Oliver. He said I could trust you. What all did he tell you?"

"Just that he thought you had seen the argument between the man who had been killed and another man. He wanted me to find out if it was the same argument, I guess." I didn't think there was any harm in saying that much.

Karl smiled. "Joe and I go way back. We were at Quantico together."

"Quantico?" I knew that was the Marine Corps base in Virginia where the FBI had their academy. "You mean. . . ."

89

"Yep. Special Agent Frank Vondra, at your service. Karl McMillian is my alias."

The revelation was a little hard to comprehend since I'd seen the man acting out just a few moments ago. My skepticism must have been evident.

"The inebriated idiot routine is just part of my cover. I'm as sober as you are." He punctuated his words with a smile and wink. "Anyway, Joe says you're okay and won't dime me out. Call me Karl, anyway, so my real name doesn't accidentally slip, okay?"

Flattered that Joe would vouch for me with such important information, I told him his secret was safe. Karl responded with a curt nod. "The guy who was found dead at Bear Butte," Karl indicated the monument in the distance, "he got into it with a guy the night before he was found."

"What do you mean?"

"Look, I'm not working the murder, so I don't know that much," Karl began. "But I can tell you that at some point before his body was found, he was in a fight with a guy at the Mato Paha Campground."

I nodded. "I was told Robert was protecting a woman."

Karl squinted as if he had just tasted something sour. "I've seen men fight over women. What I saw wasn't just about a woman."

"What do you mean?"

He cocked his head to the side, as if trying to decide how much to tell me. "Every society has it's rules, it's norms. The hardcore biker world isn't any different; they have rules, just like the rest of society."

"Rules? For the outlaw bikers?"

Karl chuckled, which was an unusually pleasant sound coming from someone who looked like he was on the other side of the law. "You aren't from around here, are you?"

"No. I've only lived here about a year. What's that got to do with anything?"

"Most of these guys," he said, indicating to the crowd of motorcycle riders lingering around, "aren't hardcore. They're doctors and engineers. This is a week of dress up for them."

I hadn't really thought about the Black Hills Motorcycle Classic as a time for adults to pretend to be something they weren't, but it did make a strange bit of sense.

Karl continued. "A very small percentage of people here, however, are the hardcore bikers: gang members, thugs, miscreants. But they still have rules that bind their subsection of society."

"Okay. . . ." I was unsure where he was going with the explanation.

He must have understood my confusion. "My point is that even the scum of normal society has rules that they follow: even if the rules seem skewed to the rest of us."

"What does this have to do with the fight?"

"Everything."

Before the undercover agent could explain, a uniformed officer who looked barely out of his teens wandered past. Karl snarled and let forth a string of profanity. The officer quickly asked if I was alright before heading on his way. When we were again alone, Karl smiled and said, "The young ones are fun to mess with."

Ignoring his comment, I urged him to continue. Thunder boomed in the distance and I noticed that the wind had picked up.

"Anyway, there are specific rules about treating women. There's even a hierarchy of women in the biker world. Remember, we're talking the hardcore, outlaw gangs, here. Not the majority, but the stereotype." He paused, searching my face for a reaction. "For the most part, women are considered property. So for someone to stick up for a woman is a big deal. It's almost unheard of."

"You told me most of these guys aren't the hardcore bikers. So what difference does it make? I don't think Robert was one."

"The other guy was."

Hesitant to admit my confusion, I remained silent.

Karl rolled his eyes. "An outlaw biker wouldn't mess with just any woman. Unless it was for a specific reason. There are enough sheep around the clubhouses for that kinda stuff."

"Sheep?" I didn't want to know what farm animals had to do with outlaw motorcycle gangs; it sounded like the set up line for a tasteless joke.

"Women who get. . .passed around."

"Oh!" I didn't want to know any more and said a silent prayer my daughters would never choose that type of life for themselves.

Karl continued. "So, my opinion, is that either there's something about that woman, or the guy who started the fight wanted a reaction from your victim."

He let out another loud string of profanities, slipping back into his previous persona so quickly that it shocked me. Confusion set in until I saw a group of people walking past.

Alone again, I asked, "Do you know who it was that started the fight?"

Karl shook his head. "I've seen him around, but I don't know him. He's in a rival gang, but he's not a big player."

"How do you know?"

"Trust me. I know." His matter-of-fact tone discouraged any further questions on the subject.

"Do you know how to find him? Anything that might help?"

He shrugged. "Not much. What I do know about the guy is that he's just here for the classic. He wears the colors and the patches, so he's in the gang at least far enough to know how the cops and lawyers work. He usually maintains a pretty low profile, but he seems well connected. My guess—and this is just a guess, mind you—is that he's a front for the money. The guy probably has a legit, or mostly legit, business where the gang can funnel drug money in and out. A position like that would give him enough rank to know how things work, but keep him far enough from whatever the bosses do that they don't get burned if something should happen to him. He probably—again, a guess—has some civilian employees mixed with some wannabes and one or two full-fledge members of the gang just to keep up appearances on all ends."

"That's a lot of work," I commented, shaking my head.

"It's harder to live outside the law than most people think. The wannabes stick around to get inside the gang. The full-fledge members keep an eye on their investments," he said the last word as if it were especially distasteful. "Finally, the civilians keep the whole operation looking legit on the surface. Everyone plays a role whether they know it or not."

As if to punctuate his words, another clap of thunder rang out overhead. Large flat drops of rain landed on the hood and roof of the car with an audible splat. I looked worriedly out the window in time to see a picturesque bolt of lightning dance off in the distance.

Karl also took notice of the worsening weather. "Storm's moving in fast. I wouldn't want to be riding in this."

Mother Nature again emphasized his words with a clap of thunder.

"Look, I've probably bored you enough. Especially since I don't have a lot of information that's helpful. Find the woman the fight was over. She may not know who was hassling her, but it's a place to start."

"What did the other guy look like?" It was something I'd forgotten to ask Judy earlier.

"Late 40s, early 50s. Fairly tall. Bald. Tanned. I'll do a composite and give it to Joe. But find the woman. She was younger, like in her 20s. If she's a sheep, she'll clam up. If she's not, she might be willing to help."

"I might know who it was," I said, thinking of Brittany. "I already gave her contact information to Joe and he's going to talk with her."

Karl shook his head. "You'll have better luck. No matter how hard Joe tries, he has trouble loosing that authoritative cop demeanor. If the woman is even slightly involved, he won't have any luck. You find her."

Lightening flashed and the thunder followed almost immediately.

"I'll see what else I can find out about the guy," Karl continued, unfazed by the storm. "I'd know him again if I saw him and, believe me, I'll find him."

"Will you call me when you find him?" Skeptical, I didn't see how that plan would work.

Karl laughed and crossed his arms. "Nah. I'll get a message to Joe."

"Hey, weren't you handcuffed?"

Karl dangled the cuffs off one wrist. "Don't you know that

appearances can be deceiving?"

I thanked him for the information as my car pulled into the parking lot and stopped a few spaces away. Joe got out and headed our direction.

As I reached for the door handle, Karl spoke once again. "Good luck. These are some bad ass dudes. Be careful."

I nodded and bolted out into the ice cold rain, Joe tossing me my keys as we passed. "Call me when you get into the car," he said, bolting for the safety of the SUV I'd just exited.

Although my car was only a few yards away, I was soaked to the bone by the time I reached it. I started the car and quickly switched the temperature gauge from air conditioning to heat. A few napkins from a recent trip to a fast food joint were laying in the backseat and I used them to soak up whatever water they would hold. When I looked up, the SUV was gone. Making a mental note to clean out the car, I dialed Joe's cell phone as once again thunder boomed overhead.

"Did you find out anything useful?" Joe didn't bother with a greeting.

"Maybe," I answered honestly. "I don't really know."

Joe grunted. "Nothing, huh? Well, it was a long shot."

"I didn't say that." I took a deep breath. I had so much information floating around my brain, I was having trouble sorting it all out, let alone trying to explain it to the intimidating FBI agent. "He gave me some information, I'm just not sure what's important at this point."

"Understood." As usual, Joe's curt tone conveyed efficiency and authority. It highlighted Karl's observation about Joe's "cop demeanor" more than anything. "Look, I'm going to be tied up in town for a bit. Is there anything you need from me right away or can you take this new information and run with it?"

What I really wanted to do was go home, put on some dry clothes, and curl up with a good book. Instead of mentioning that, however, I mumbled an agreement.

"I guess I'll go find Judy's friend, then," I said referring to the flower seller I'd met earlier.

Joe and I made arrangements to meet up a few hours later before he disconnected the call with the same efficient professionalism he normally conveyed. I realized I'd forgotten to tell him that Karl was going to have a composite sketch of the man fighting with Robert. Then again, Karl was a law enforcement officer, so he probably already told Joe that.

Mostly dry thanks to the heater of my car, I took a few moments to contemplate my next move. Not for the first time, I regretted my involvement with the FBI. I wasn't a police officer, nor did I have any desire to be one.

The park and nearby street were almost devoid of people and bikes. Everyone was probably seeking shelter from the wind and rain which was still falling heavily. Bear Butte loomed in the distance like a silent sentinel.

Above the geological laccolith, dark storm clouds consolidated to form the image of another bear; this one large, menacing, and angry.

Chapter Seventeen

I studied the clouds in the distance. A large bear formed by thunderclouds above a Lakota sacred site named Bear Butte? Where a murder had occurred? It didn't take a genius to read that sign.

I needed to know more about the argument at the campground. To do that I needed to find someone who had witnessed it. The only person I knew who fit the bill was Judy's friend, Brittany.

How was I supposed to find one person—a person who I'd never met before, let alone seen from a distance—in a place as transient as the classic? The cliché about finding a needle in a haystack suddenly made a lot of sense. Even without a plan, I headed back to the campground searching for answers. Hopefully, the place was still crawling with police.

I tried to remember details about the crowd I'd seen at the campground when I first arrived. I honestly hadn't been paying that much attention to the throng of people, being more focused on trying to find Joe in the semi-organized chaos. Picturing the scene wasn't helping and I could feel my teeth start to grind together in frustration. A decade earlier I probably would have let out a string of profanities, but I had made a conscious effort to clean up my language after Zach parroted one of my more frustrating moments when he was a toddler. Now I stuck to clenching my jaw and grinding my teeth—much to my dentist's dismay. Taking a deep breath, I exhaled slowly, willing the tension and frustration to exit with my breath.

The rainstorm had passed quickly, although it left large puddles in its wake. Ground that had been hard packed dust that morning transformed into a mud pie chef's fantasy kitchen in little under two hours. My kids would have had a field day. The biker crowd at the campground, however, didn't seem amused.

As I watched, the campground area again came alive with activity. People who had sought shelter in nylon tents began to venture out and those who hadn't made it to the campground before the storm hit were beginning to arrive. With all the activity taking place before my eyes, finding one mysterious young lady seemed like an even more daunting task. I ran my hand through my long, curly, reddish hair. Still chilled from being caught briefly in the rain, my clothes had mostly dried. Sweltering heat and an ice cold rain shower in the same day; South Dakota's weather was something I didn't think I would ever get used to.

Closing my eyes, I took another deep breath. I knew I was avoiding the idea of trying to find out any information. My heart wasn't in it. At least last time I got involved I had a reason to find the killer. Not this time. This time I was sticking my nose where it didn't belong.

The moment the thought was formed, I knew I wasn't alone.

"Justice is everyone's business, *Cuwitku.*" He Who Waits sounded tired, if a spirit could be tired. He had manifested himself in the passenger's seat beside me. His leather pants and beaded shirt were opaque, adding to the overall drained effect.

Had he been flesh and blood, I would have suggested a long nap. Instead I acknowledged his words with a short nod, but remained silent. Even though I was safely alone in my car, I didn't feel comfortable speaking aloud. Since no one else could see the shaman, I wanted to avoid the appearance of talking to myself like some crazy woman if anyone happened to be watching.

Again reading my thoughts, He Who Waits began to chastise me. "What others think should be of no concern to you. Do the deer concern themselves with the affairs of the buffalo? Or the sparrow with that of the trout?"

When I didn't answer, he continued. "Each is concerned with themselves; with what they must do. For they know that only in doing their part will their destiny be fulfilled."

"Yes, but—"

He cut me off. "There is no but. When a person, like an animal, does not follow destiny, there is an imbalance in nature. Humans, much like their animal brothers and sisters, must follow their nature."

Knowing I'd been beat, I took a deep sigh before agreeing with his statements. "I am trying, you know."

It was his turn to nod. "I am aware. You have journeyed a great distance."

Mentally translating his formal speech into *You've come a long way*, I quickly thanked him before attempting to change the subject. There are two things I don't do well. One of them is accept a compliment. The other is ask for help. I went two for two. "What do I do now? I don't feel like I'm any closer to finding answers about Robert's death. I'm not sure what direction to go at all. There are so many people here and so few who probably know anything. I'm not even sure how to find people who might be helpful. I . . . I need some help."

I'd given similar speeches to He Who Waits in the past and they'd never done any good. This time, however, I was surprised to find that my voice didn't reach the whiney pitch it had in the past nor the resigned tone I'd used after reaching the conclusion that whiny wasn't going to work. I felt proud that I had at least learned one lesson from working with my spirit guide.

"The girl will seek you out." He Who Waits sounded confident, so I chose not to question him. Although, her finding me seemed just as laborious as my tracking her down. Talking to Brittany, however, probably wasn't going to lead me straight to the killer and time was running out.

As he had done in the past, He Who Waits read my thoughts. "You are correct; time is of the essence."

"Great," I mumbled. "No pressure from beyond."

The shaman looked at me, his eyebrow raised in an unspoken question.

"Sorry." I shook my head and rolled my shoulders. "This is a little stressful, you know."

He Who Waits nodded, but remained silent. Outside the vehicle, more motorcycle riders had arrived at the campground and the rain had almost completely evaporated or been soaked into the dry earth. Only the most remote spots and the deepest potholes showed any signs of the earlier storm. Experience told me the humidity was waiting to wreak havoc on my curls.

"You are willing to accept some parts of destiny with more ease than others, are you not?"

I wasn't sure how to take that, so I kept quiet.

He Who Waits stayed silent as well.

It wasn't long before my impatience got the better of me. "Wouldn't it be easier for you to just tell me who killed Robert? Or get a message to Joe another way? I don't imagine this is much easier for you than it is for me."

Those questions remained unanswered; He Who Waits had again vanished.

I didn't have time to ponder the questions myself, not that I would have come up with any answers, because my cell phone began to ring. I didn't recognize the number on the screen, so I was both professional and hesitant in answering.

The voice on the other end of the line sounded young and nervous. "Um, I'm trying to reach a lady named Cerri."

"This is Cerri." I couldn't place the voice, but knew she couldn't be a telemarketer. They never managed to get my name right.

"My name is Brittney. You talked with my friend Judy today and she asked me to give you a call."

Chapter Eighteen

Yes, He Who Waits had told me the girl would find me. I hadn't expected her to call less than five minutes later.

The phone conversation with Brittany was short. She had called from a nearby bar. It was a classic hotspot I recognized for its loud concerts and rowdy reputation. Even this early in the day, I could barely hear her over the background noise. We agreed to meet at the lemonade stand where I'd sat with Judy earlier.

I started the car and pulled out onto the main road leading back toward the actual town. It was only a few miles from the campground to Main Street, and the drive took longer than it would have taken me to walk it. Well, maybe not, but it sure seemed like it since traffic was slow. I used the time to check in at home, making sure Matt knew where I was and reassuring myself that the kids were fine. As I approached Main Street, traffic crawled almost to a standstill as motorcycles were allowed to continue, but all other vehicles were diverted to side streets. I decided to head toward to the same parking lot I'd used earlier. I wasn't going to attempt to find a free parking spot since so many of the other public parking areas that had been almost empty earlier in the day now boasted signs reading "Lot Full." I didn't have much faith that I'd be able to get a spot any closer than the campground I'd just left, but traffic made it impossible to turn back.

I finally made my way to the same church parking lot I'd been to earlier. Surprised they still had space, I gratefully pulled into the parking lot and maneuvered into the spot the attendant pointed to.

Always rather frugal, I didn't like the idea of paying to park in the same place, but I didn't see any other option. I grabbed some cash out of my wallet as I walked toward the attendant.

When I handed the money to the attendant, he didn't take it. "You were here earlier, right?"

I nodded.

"Thought so. Did you find the guy giving out the pins you were asking about?"

"Um, no. Well, sort of. I saw the Bone's Bikes booth but I didn't see any more pins. I can't believe you remembered that."

The attendant shrugged. "It wasn't all that busy during the rainstorm. Besides, most people just pay the cash and are on the way. Very few strike up a conversation. Makes it easier to remember those who do."

He still hadn't taken my money. "How much to park?"

"Don't worry about it. It's the same price for all day. You weren't gone that long and we have the space." He held up his hand with the palm toward me. "Consider this my random act of kindness for the day."

Before I even had a chance to thank him, he turned and walked away.

Still amazed at my good fortune, I headed for my meeting with Brittany.

It didn't take me long to reach the same lemonade stand that I'd visited earlier. Part of me hoped that the wood picnic tables would be full so that I didn't need to risk a splinter. On the other hand, sitting at a table would make communication easier. I could almost hear my mother's Irish lilt saying "Cerridwen, lass, sometimes you have to take a risk to get what you want. Life isn't about playing it safe, you know."

The stand was only a few blocks away and didn't take me long to get there. Either there were fewer people roaming the streets or I had become more accustomed to the crowd. There was no line at the lemonade stand, which made me glad. I was afraid that I wouldn't be able to find Brittany in the crowd. Instead, when I approached the stand, there was only one person standing in line.

I slowed my pace so that I could study the young woman, who I recognized from when I had literally bumped into Judy earlier. At first glance Brittany looked small and frail. But as I got closer, I realized she wasn't either. She was shorter than I was by at least a few inches, but at 5'9" I was used to being among the group of taller women. Her long, straight, blond hair was pulled back into a pony tail, emphasizing her lean face. She was so thin that I assumed she needed to put rocks in her pocket when South Dakota's winds kicked in. In her summer clothes, however, it was clear that she could hold her own; her biceps and calves had definitions that would have made a teenage boy jealous.

When I was within ten feet of her, she spoke. "You Cerri?" Her voice was high pitched with just a hint of laughter underneath that reached all the way into her blue-green eyes. I could imagine her breaking out into a fit of giggles at the slightest opportunity. Between her kind eyes and her girl-next-door beauty, I imagined the boys overlooked her muscular frame for the opportunity to be near her.

I held out my hand and introduced myself. After ordering, I grabbed some napkins and the drinks and made my way to where Brittany was waiting at the same picnic table Judy and I had sat at earlier.

"Thanks," she said as she took the lemonade I offered her. No lady-like sips for her, she took long, deep draws that made me wonder if she even tasted the tart liquid.

"You're welcome." As I gingerly sat on the dry wood, I wasn't sure how to start the conversation. I didn't think I would get a lot of information if I waited for my companion to spill her guts. Deciding it was best to jump right in, I said, "I appreciate you calling me. I wasn't sure you would."

Brittany shrugged. "Almost didn't."

One of the best skills a journalist can hone is the ability to read the people being interviewed and I called upon that talent as I searched her face and found complete honesty, despite a touch of fear. Upon careful scrutiny, I decided she looked as nervous as I felt. I remained silent, wondering how to get the conversation headed in the direction I needed it to without spooking her into silence.

Before I had a chance to ask what she meant, Brittany continued.

"But Judy told me you were cool. A little strange, but cool."

Considering the girls' ages, I took that as a compliment. "Judy said you saw the man who was killed. At the campground."

Brittany nodded. She took the plastic lid off her cup and set it on the wooden table. Tipping the cup back, she took a mouthful of ice before setting the cup back on the table. I briefly considered telling her how bad chewing ice was for her teeth and then decided that bit of motherly-advice would show my age and possibly end the interview before I found out anything useful. Besides, with my own teeth grinding habit, I didn't think I was the best spokesperson for dental hygiene. And no one hates a hypocrite more than a teenager.

She chewed the ice, but remained silent.

"Do you mind telling me what happened?"

She shrugged again and I wondered how that age group ever had a conversation if shrugs were so common. Still relying on my journalistic training, I waited for her to speak. I didn't have to wait long.

"It's probably not important, but sure. I'll tell you." Brittany took a deep breath and another mouthful of ice. She continued speaking as the ice melted into her mouth, stopping her description every so often to swallow. "A couple nights ago Judy and I were hanging around the campground after work. We were talking and laughing with some guys a few sites over. They seemed okay. Kinda badass, but they weren't flying colors or anything."

I interrupted. "They weren't in a gang? You're sure."

Another shrug. "Pretty sure. I mean, people aren't supposed to fly their colors at the campground, but they do anyway. Or they have patches on their jackets or vests or whatever." She poured more ice into her mouth. "Plus, these guys were younger. Like twenty-two or something. Not old. And they were pretty cool, ya know?"

Even I knew that motorcycle gangs were comprised of men in their late teens and early twenties, but I remained silent.

"So we were hanging with them, having a good time, sitting around the campfire bull sh. . .um, talking, ya know?" She glanced at me, as if she hoped I hadn't realized what she had been going to say. "It was still early—like 10:30 or 11 and things were still pretty quiet."

By 11 p.m. I'm usually ready for bed, but I didn't stop Brittany from continuing her story.

"So we're just chillaxin' and waiting for the things to get started when these three really intense guys showed up."

"Chillaxin'? Intense?" I felt like she had started speaking a foreign language.

"Chilling out. Relaxing. You know, chillaxin'. And intense. Like totally hard core. Real scary dudes."

"Got it."

"Anyway, we're chillaxin' and these guys show up and sit right down, making themselves at home like they were invited. And they were smashed, too. You could smell the alcohol on them." Brittany closed her eyes and shivered at the memory. "Judy had gone back to our cabin to get something. She was supposed to be coming right back, but hadn't yet. One of them sat down next to me. Every time I moved over, he did too. It was awkward. Really, really awkward."

Brittany's words were coming faster and she started breathing deeper. When she paused for another mouthful of ice, I patted her hand in reassurance.

After a moment she continued. "So the guys we were with, one of them told the other guys to get lost. But they wouldn't leave. We tried ignoring them, but that didn't work either."

"Go on."

"Finally, I got up to leave. I figured that I'd go back to the cabin and get Judy. I just wanted to get outta there, ya know?"

I nodded.

"So I stand up and the guy next me grabs my arm and pulls me back down saying something like 'where you going, baby?' I just wanted to get outta there." She paused again, taking a deep breath before progressing with her story. A hint of shame had crept into her eyes as if she was embarrassed that she'd managed to get herself into such a precarious situation. "Well, I must have screamed out or something. I don't remember doing that, but Judy said she heard me all the way at our cabin, or maybe she was headed back by then, I'm not sure. Either way, the next thing I know this other guy—the guy who got killed—"

"Robert?"

"Yeah, him. He shows up and tells the hard core jerks to scram. The guy who grabbed me—I don't remember his name, I don't think he ever said it—told the new guy he wasn't going anywhere and then the new guy said 'wanna bet?' By then, the guy had let go of my arm and I was backing away from the campsite. The guys we'd been hanging out with, they were all standing up and the other guys were all standing up and it looked a fight was about to break out."

"And it did, right?" I asked when she paused.

Brittany nodded. "Yep. Only it wasn't between the groups of guys. The guy who had been messing with me, he walked up to that Robert guy and got all in his face. Yelling and screaming and acting all tough. Robert, he just stood there. I don't think he ever raised his voice much above a whisper. The other guy really didn't like that and kept screaming. He was getting louder and louder. I thought the cops or security or someone was going to show up, but they didn't. At least not then. Instead, Robert said something else—I was too far away by then to hear and, like I said, he was talking really quiet—and then turned around and started to walk away. That's when the drunk guy went after Robert. He sucker punched him and the fight was on."

I could tell she was done with her story. Relief began to replace the fear in her eyes and her breathing had slowed to a more natural rhythm. It amazed me how naive and vulnerable she seemed and wondered why her parents let her spend the week at the classic. I kept my opinion to myself, however, not knowing if I would need more information from her later. If I was going to need to talk with her again, it would be better if it was a pleasant experience, another rule from my journalism background. Aloud I asked, "How did the fight go?"

Brittany reverted back to shrugging. "Dunno. Didn't stick around long enough to watch. Those one guys gave me the creeps. I looked for that Robert guy later, to thank him, ya know. But he wasn't around."

"I thought Judy said he had stayed at the same campground you two did."

"I'm pretty sure he did. I mean, I'd seen him around. On the way to the toilet and all that, but I'd never talked to him before that night. Never had a reason to." Brittany lowered her eyes. "Like I said, I looked for him later, but couldn't find him. I really wanted to thank him, ya know?"

When she glanced back at me, I saw the guilt had returned to her eyes. "You aren't responsible for his death, Brittany."

Her eyes began to water and her voice wavered. "You don't know that."

She was right. I didn't. I had no idea why someone killed Robert. But I wasn't going to tell her that. Instead, I reached over to touch her hand once again.

We sat that way for a few minutes, listening to the roar of motorcycles cruising up and down Main Street. It was Brittany who spoke first. "I know. I know I didn't kill him or anything. But . . . ."

"But what if he was killed because he stuck up for you? Is that what you think?"

She nodded, silent tears running down her cheeks.

"You didn't kill him." I stressed the first word. "Someone else did. Someone else made that decision. Not you."

Brittany sniffled as she nodded in agreement. I was struck by how vulnerable she looked and said a silent prayer that she would release her undeserved guilt.

"I'm sorry, Brittany, but I do have a few other questions for you."

"I told you everything," she said, the false bravado causing her voice to waiver slightly. "I really don't know anything else."

"You never know what small detail may be important." I had read that in some mystery novel and it sounded good then. When the words came out of my mouth, however, they sounded hollow. I hoped Brittany wouldn't notice. "The guys who crashed your party. You didn't get any names?"

She shook her head, but remained silent.

"Have you seen them around the campground? Did you notice anything that would help identify them?"

"There are a lot of people at that campground," Brittany said. "A lot of people. I can't be sure. But I'm pretty sure they're staying there. Not near the cabin where Judy and I are, but I think they've been around. And these guys, they aren't doctors and lawyers playing dress up. They're the real deal."

Great. Official scary motorcycle gang members. When I finished talking with Brittany, I would call Joe and go home.

No way was I going to get involved with people Karl had told me about.

No way was I going to put myself or my family in danger.

No way.

Brittany must have taken my silence as encouragement to continue. "I told you I think they're staying at the same campground, right? Well, if I'm right, they were wearing Hell's Outlaw patches on their vests. I mean, I can't be positive, but I think it was them. And if they're HOs, then, well, I guess they could have killed that guy." Her voice had started to waiver again. "Just because he stuck up for me."

"I'm sure there was more to it than that," I replied. "If those are the people involved. And that's a big if right now."

She sniffled. "So, the police don't know who's responsible?"

Not knowing how to answer that question, I changed the subject.

"How could I find these guys?" I really didn't want to find them. They could stay lost for all I cared, but I doubted I'd get off that easily with either Joe or He Who Waits.

Brittany remained quiet, her eyebrows scrunching together in concentration. "One of the guys had a bunch of tats. But that's probably not much help, is it?"

I shrugged. "Where any of them unique?"

"Not really. I remember one of the other guys, not the one bugging me, he had something on each of his fingers. I never could tell what, though."

"Brittany, do you think that you'd recognize any of the guys if you saw them again? I mean, without a doubt?"

It was her turn to shrug. "Probably."

This conversation didn't seem to be going anywhere, and I didn't think I was any closer to finding the killer than I was before talking to the young woman.

I prepared to tell her goodbye when a change came over her. If she had been a cartoon, I would have seen a light bulb go off above Brittany's head. As it was, she broke out into a smile that reached all the way to her eyes, transforming her face and adding a twinkle that hadn't been there previously. "I have an idea."

In her enthusiasm, I was reminded just how young she was. I may not have been old enough to be her mother, but I could have been her much older sister. I didn't want anything to happen to her because of the questions I was asking. "What?"

"I have a sketch."

I looked at my companion in amazement. "A sketch?"

She nodded. "I'm an art student. Drawing helps me process things. So, afterward, I made a sketch of the creep who was bugging me. I, um, brought it with me if you think it would help. I don't need it anymore."

She handed me a folded piece of paper. "It's what I remember."

Amazed at my good fortune, I took the paper, opened it and glanced at the drawing of the man. I didn't recognize him, and some of the facial features seemed slightly skewed, but I didn't want to hurt Brittany's feelings. Maybe Joe could find a use for it.

"Thank you. I'm sure this will help."

"Hey, Brit-Brat, let's go. We're going to be late." The voice's owner, a stocky young man of around Brittany's age with shaggy brown hair and large blue eyes, approached.

When she saw him, Brittany stood up. "My boyfriend. I told him to meet me here. In case you were, you know, a crazy lady, or something."

I smiled. "Good idea. You can't be too careful."

As they disappeared into the crowd, I hoped her sketch would help.

Chapter Nineteen

By the time I made it back to Rapid City, thoughts of bikers and murder and undercover agents had gotten so jumbled in my mind that untangling the mess of necklaces in the girls' jewelry boxes would have been easier. A quick phone call home and it was decided pizza was for dinner.

"Ya know, I could cook when I get home," I told Matt.

"Yes. Or you could pick up a pizza." His whisper was overly exaggerated and I could hear squeals of delight in the background.

"What kind do you want?"

Matt chuckled. "Not only do I know exactly what we want, I already called. It should be waiting for you."

It was my turn to laugh. "Good thing I called you then, isn't it?"

"Yeah it is. The kids would have staged a mutiny if you walked in empty handed. I'm sure of it. Besides, I was getting ready to call you, anyway."

"A mutiny, huh?"

"Armed with water balloon grenades and multiple super soakers. I should know. I've been filling their ammo for an hour."

"You better figure out how to get that ammo back before I show up with the pizza, or you'll end up drinking your pepperoni."

"I don't think we'll have to worry about that," Matt said. "Zach is almost empty again and it's only a matter of time before Kenzie and Maddie finish him off. They don't know it yet, but I'll cut their supply lines."

"Aren't you the tricky one?"

"They never suspect the supply clerk."

"Okay, crazy man. I'm at the pizza place. I'll be home soon."

"Drive safe. Love you."

"Love you, too, and I will. Promise." It was our standard telephone goodbye and falling into the routine helped put the craziness I'd experienced during the rest of my day into perspective: an island of sanity in a world of crazy. Saying the words was like a cloud had been lifted from my shoulders.

I had barely gotten back into the car with the pizza when my cell phone rang. This time I made sure to check the caller ID screen before answering.

Agent Joe Oliver.

"Hi, Joe." I hoped I didn't sound as frustrated as I felt. I wasn't ever going to feel comfortable talking with the FBI. It wasn't something normal, non-law enforcement people did on a regular basis and twice in twelve months seemed much too regular for me.

"Cerri." He said my name like a statement. "I'm glad I caught you. Are you busy?"

"Well, I'm headed home with dinner." As soon as the words were out of my mouth, my stomach growled. The rumbling was so loud I was sure it could be heard on the other end of the phone.

Either my stomach wasn't as loud as I feared, or Joe was being polite. He didn't mention the noise. "I really hate to impose, and I know you're helping me out as a favor, but is there a way I could meet you? Maybe at your house? I don't want to keep you from your dinner, but…"

For a split second I considered declining; telling him that I was going to go home, scarf down a few slices of pizza with my husband and children, and possibly veg out in front of the television or play an invigorating game of Go Fish with the kids. The one thing not on my agenda was to think about death or murder or bikers or the FBI. Before I could say any of that, however, I remembered my mother and her natural hospitality. When I was growing up, one of her favorite sayings had been "Hospitality is making your guests feel at home, even if you wish they were."

I knew I'd be sharing our dinner with the FBI agent.

Perhaps I hesitated a moment too long because Joe said, "I understand it's an imposition and I wouldn't normally just invite myself over for dinner—"

"No, it's fine," I interrupted. "We're just having pizza. There will be plenty. You don't mind pepperoni, do you?"

"Love it," Joe replied. "But you're sure it won't be an imposition?" There was a note of hesitation in his voice. Or else I was so tired and stressed by my day of investigating that I was imagining things.

"It's not a problem at all," I assured him. "Really, there will be plenty."

"Well, okay. It would make things easier."

I didn't ask what would be easier over pizza with Matt and the kids around. I didn't really want to know.

We made arrangements for Joe to meet at the house. It was decided that we'd eat first and then I would share what I'd learned.

After hanging up with Joe, I quickly called Matt and let him know to expect one more. As I pulled into our subdivision, I wondered how anything ever got done before cell phones and was simultaneously annoyed and grateful that driving and talking was still legal.

By the time I made it to the house, the smell of pizza permeated the air in my car. My stomach had given up it's occasional growling, and resorted to loud and continuous rumbling.

With far less grace than a circus acrobat, I managed to get me, the pizzas and my purse out of the car in one trip without spilling anything. As I was trying to open the front door, still balancing purse and pizzas, I heard a car pull into the driveway.

"Hold on. Let me get the door for you." Joe called to me before he shut his own car door.

I considered telling Joe not to worry about it, that I could manage. However, heat from the pizza had already transferred through the cardboard box and had started to scald my forearm as I balanced the boxes like an old-fashioned waiter. Despite all the excitement I'd heard earlier, it seemed my family had forgotten to be available to help carry the load. The situation irked me for no real reason.

"Must be the kinda day I've had," I mumbled under my breath.

I must have spoken louder than I thought, because Joe looked at me strangely. "I'm sorry, what?"

"Never mind."

Joe gawked a moment longer before reaching around me and opening the screen door and turning the knob to open the oak front door, however, he remained silent.

Nichole R. Bennett

We barely made it inside the house before I understood why no one was waiting to open the door: the twins were trying to play a board game while their older brother succeeded in bothering them, running and taking a leap over where the girls were sprawled out on the living room floor. The noise of the girls' protests combined with Zach's laughter and ridicule to make the living room louder than most school gymnasiums. Matt was nowhere to be seen and I assumed he was hiding out in the basement. It wouldn't have been the first time he hid when he was supposed to be watching the children.

Whether it was the noise of us entering the house or the smell of the pizza, Zach was the first to notice us. "Pizza!"

His yells were matched by the girls, who jumped up, scattering the game board and pieces. It wasn't going to be easy to continue the game with the mess they had made. In the midst of the chaos, Matt joined us first in the living room and followed the procession into the kitchen, where the Zach set paper plates on the table and the girls got napkins and cups for everyone.

Matt and Joe stood off to the side, talking quietly. I couldn't hear what they were talking about, but Joe's solemn, curt nod made me think Matt was warning the FBI agent about various conversations the children shouldn't hear.

If Matt was stern with our visitor, the kids were curious. Although none of the kids actually spoke to our visitor—other than polite hellos, that is—they all stole glances both to the mountain of a man and to each other.

Once we'd all sat down to the enticing pizza, their curiosity got the better of them.

Kenzie was the first to speak. "Are you a teacher like Daddy?"

"No," Joe replied slowly, casting a glance at Matt before proceeding. "I'm a police officer."

That was enough to open the flood gates. The rest of our meal was filled with questions about Joe's occupation from Zach—*can I see your badge and your gun* and *have you ever shot anyone*—and questions about Joe's personal life from the girls—*are you married* and *do you have any kids*.

112

To his credit, Joe answered the questions the kids threw at him with both grace and tact. He had obviously fielded questions from kids before.

By the time dinner was finished, Joe had found himself three new fans. Not one of the kids wanted to do much more than sit and talk with him.

"Go on now," Matt said. "The grownups need to talk."

Mattie, Kenzie and Zach exchanged worried glances. It wasn't often that we asked the children to leave.

"It's okay, guys," Joe reassured them.

Each face looked anxious, but the kids left the room without another word.

Matt stood to leave as well.

"Wait." Joe's voice was quiet, but firm. "You might as well stay. I've broken enough rules and regulations as it is."

I shot Joe a questioning glance, but remained silent.

Matt sat back down, glancing between the FBI Agent and me. None of us spoke.

After what seemed to be an eternity, Joe cleared his throat. "I really appreciate your help, Cerri."

"Well," I began, "I'm not sure anything I have to say is going to be much help."

I told Joe the things I'd learned, being careful not to mention that some of the information came from fairies. He had been tolerant about how I knew things before, but I didn't think fairies were something he could easily accept. I still wasn't sure their existence was something I could accept and I saw them with my own eyes.

He asked few questions as I spoke, though he took copious notes.

When I was finished, the three of us sat silent once again, each lost in our own thoughts.

Matt was the first to speak. "Do you think that the tattoo could be a Day of the Dead skull?"

Joe looked at my husband. "What's that?"

"The Day of the Dead is a Mexican holiday. It's a day to honor those who have passed away," Matt explained. "I'm pretty sure it's celebrated on November 1st. But one of the traditions includes decorated sugar skulls."

Something about Matt's explanation sounded familiar. "Are those the ones with the frosting all over them?"

Matt nodded. "I've been seeing more tattoos on my students the past few years, and I've seen those skulls a few times. Maybe you're looking for someone with a tattoo like that?"

"It must be a popular image right now. I saw those things a few different places." I stood and held up my finger to signal that the men should wait. I went to my purse and dug past a mess of other papers to find the pamphlet I'd picked up at the rally. When I returned to the table, I handed the brochure to Joe. "There's even a custom bike company that uses the skull as part of their design."

Joe looked at the information I'd handed him. "Bone's Bikes. Never heard of them."

I remained silent, since the only motorcycle company I could name before being sucked into this investigation was a Harley.

The FBI Agent glanced up at me. "Can I keep this?"

I shrugged. "Sure. If you think it will help."

"Never know," he answered. "Did you find out anything else?"

I knew he wanted to know if some spirit or ghost had told me who the killer was. Judging by look my husband was giving me, Matt wanted to know the same thing.

Taking a deep breath I said, "Only that I did find witnesses to the fight. The girls gave me a sketch of the man Robert was fighting with."

Joe's eyebrows raised, but he didn't say anything.

"What fight?" Matt asked.

Joe explained about the fight at the campground while I watched the two men. Joe's face had been more expressive during this conversation than I had ever seen it before and I wondered if it was difficult for him to maintain his cop face all the time. I couldn't do it.

When he was finished, Joe turned to me. "How did you find any witnesses?"

"It was. . .a coincidence. I bumped into someone. Literally."

"And the sketch?"

"Brittany is studying art, from what I understand. She made a sketch of the guy who was bothering her at the campground. The one Robert had a fight with. She gave me the sketch when I talked to her today. Remind me to get it for you before you leave. I'm sure it will be more helpful to you than to me."

Joe and Matt both looked skeptical.

"Hey, it might work," I justified. "It's better than nothing, anyway."

"It is," Joe agreed. He took a deep breath before continuing. "At least we have some new directions to go in. And we can compare her sketch to the one Karl did this afternoon."

Hesitantly, I asked, "Are you having any luck on your end?"

He shrugged. "I can tell you Mesmer had been an insurance agent for the past fifteen years or so. There was one man who had threatened Mesmer a month or so ago over a declined insurance claim. We're looking into that, but I don't think it's going to get us anywhere."

"Why not? Sounds like a viable suspect," Matt said.

"I don't think so," Joe replied, glancing at his notes. "The claim was for property damage. Seems the guy's business went up in flames in the middle of the night. Mesmer advised the insurance company not to pay. Said it was probably arson."

"A very viable suspect," Matt reiterated.

"Yeah, except there's no evidence the guy has left Washington State in the past six weeks."

"Of course not," I mumbled. "Couldn't be that easy, could it?"

Both men ignored my comment. Joe continued as if I hadn't spoken. "It doesn't look like the wife left Washington, either."

"Why didn't she come with him?" I couldn't imagine taking a vacation without Matt.

"According to the guys who interviewed her, she wasn't that enthused about him coming out here for the classic, especially on his bike. They had a big blow-up right before he left."

"That poor woman," I said. "She'll carry that guilt for the rest of her life."

Matt didn't say anything, but reached out and squeezed my hand.

"There is one other thing," Joe began. "You know that Mesmer had a juvie record in Louisiana. Some petty theft, disturbing the peace, that type of thing. But I verified that as an adult, his record was clean."

"Wouldn't that have been sealed or expunged or something? I mean, from when he was a kid." I knew that's what happened on television, anyway.

"It was. But he was also a possible witness to a drive by shooting in Louisiana. Eventually, the cops down there arrested someone and his possible involvement wasn't pursued."

"You mean besides the one that Lieutenant McShane told us about?" I asked.

Joe only nodded.

"How did he get from Louisiana to Washington?"

"It looks like sometime after that shooting his mother shipped him off to live with an uncle. He didn't get any more trouble after that. Not even so much as a speeding ticket."

"Sounds like he got his act together, anyway," Matt said.

Joe shrugged. "Or he just didn't get caught again."

"Little cynical?" I recognized Matt's tone as teasing, but he didn't wait long enough for Joe to respond. "Must be an occupational hazard."

In the milliseconds that followed, I was sure Joe was going to become the grade-A jerk he had been the first time I'd worked with him.

Instead he cracked a smile. "Yeah, I guess it is."

I hadn't realized I had been holding my breath until I let it out so forcefully that it caused both men to glance in my direction. "Um, is there anything else? Anything you need me to look for?"

Joe shook his head. "Honestly? I have no idea."

Matt's left eyebrow raised questioningly.

Joe turned his attention to my husband. "Maybe Cerri didn't mention it, but I'm not officially on the case. One of my good friends is the head ranger out at Bear Butte. And, of course, because of the classic, every law enforcement agency in the area is a bit short-staffed. When I heard the location of the murder, and the religious significance to the Lakota, well, I thought Cerri might have some . . .

insight similar to what she knew about the murder at Devils Tower."

Matt squeezed my hand again. "Cerri can be full of insight." His voice maintained the teasing quality it held earlier. "She manages to always know what I'm up to."

Joe let a chuckle escape his lips. "Right now my biggest concern is the tourist population. Too many people come and go during the annual bike week. Makes finding whoever did this even more difficult."

Matt and I both nod in agreement. "I'm glad it's not my job," I said before realizing the absurdity of the statement.

To cover my embarrassment, I stood and began cleaning up the remains of our dinner. The two men began to talk about the Little League World Series, which one of the Rapid City teams was gearing up to compete in. Sports didn't interest me much, so I quietly left the room and went outside on the deck.

I'm not sure how long I stayed there. It was still hot, a slight breeze had picked up and the temperature seemed more bearable. Somewhere in the neighborhood, someone had been grilling. It smelled wonderful.

The few minutes outside, quiet and alone, were enough after fighting my way through crowds most of the day. My mother would have called it something like "finding my center." Whatever the few minutes alone were called, being alone felt energizing.

Heading back into the house, I was surprised to see Joe getting ready to leave.

"Sorry," I said to him. "I was kind of a lousy hostess."

Joe shook his head. "Nah. I pretty much invited myself to dinner. I appreciate you putting up with me." He held out his hand to me, and I shook it.

"I'll give you a call if anything else comes to me," I told him.

"Sounds good," he replied. "And, Cerri, thanks again. I owe you one."

I watched him walk down the driveway, get in his car, and leave, all the time wondering what he meant. Later I realized I'd forgotten to give him the sketch.

117

Chapter Twenty

I spent the rest of that evening with Matt and the kids doing nothing in particular. When I tucked the kids into bed, however, I couldn't help but give them a hug that was just a little longer and a little tighter than usual.

If Zach noticed, he didn't comment. Maddie just looked at me strangely. Kenzie, though, mentioned it.

"What's wrong, Mommy?" she asked, her voice straining against sleep.

"Nothing, honey. I just needed to give you guys extra big hugs tonight. That's all."

"Is it because of the police man?"

A wry smile crossed my face. "Maybe a little. But I think sometimes moms just need an extra hug. Just like sometimes little girls do."

Kenzie looked thoughtfully as she tried unsuccessfully to stifle a yawn. "Okay. Do you need another one?"

"Another hug? Sure."

I got my second hug from Kenzie, kissed her forehead and told her to go to sleep. Her breathing was steady and even before I had made it to the bedroom door.

"Mommy." Maddie's voice, just as sleep-laden as Kenzie's, called to me from the other twin bed.

"I thought you were already asleep, Sugarbutt." I walked toward her.

"Would a kiss help, too?"

"Of course it would."

I collected my kiss and made it out of the twin's bedroom.

From the family room, I could hear the television, a faint rumbling too soft for me to make out any actual words. I hadn't really had time to talk about anything with Matt and I desperately needed his logical mind to put me at ease.

Matt was in the family room, as I suspected. However, there

would be no talking to him. He had made himself comfortable by stretching out in his recliner. The television was on, and he had a book face down on his chest. Muffled by the sound, his light snores were barely audible.

Years of marriage taught me not to wake him. He would tell me that he was actually reading that book, watching the television. Instead, I placed a blanket across his lap and headed toward my office figuring that I might as well work to take my mind off the events of the day.

It didn't work. I checked my e-mail and decided there was nothing that couldn't wait.

Going to bed wasn't much better. I tossed and turned for more than an hour before falling into an uneasy sleep. My dreams that night were some of the strangest I'd had in a long time: consisting of people riding motorcycles down the road but instead of normal heads, they had painted skulls devoid of flesh.

Matt had crawled into bed around midnight and I became even more conscious of my restlessness as I tried not to disturb him. Eventually, I decided to stop pretending to sleep. Putting on my robe, something I normally saved for Christmas, Easter and other mornings when cameras could be present, I started the coffee pot and waited until there was enough for a cup.

Mornings had never been my forte, making me grateful no one else was awake in the pre-dawn hours. The last thing I wanted was conversation.

Finally there was enough brown liquid to fill my "World's Greatest Mom" mug. I took the mug and headed for the back porch. Sitting in one of the patio chairs, I watched the sky as the sun began its colorful ascent over the Badlands. During the course of a normal day, I often forgot how close the subdivision was to, well, nothing. Yes, we were close to Rapid City, but also to the wilderness of the Southern Black Hills. A dog barked in the distance and I realized how quiet the neighborhood was. Deer were feeding on the horizon and a few rabbits were chasing each other in the yard.

Two rabbits began hoping over each other, playing a strange game of leap frog—leap rabbit?—as they ventured closer to where I was sitting. They looked so carefree that I envied them.

Smiling, I watched them approach, zigzagging through the grass. It wasn't until they were much closer that I noticed the slight pink undertone of one of the rabbits. In another few leaps, I could see the deep green eyes of the second one. They reminded me of something I couldn't quite place. Once the two were close enough to touch, however, I knew where I'd seen such creatures. When they started to sparkle I realized the true impact of my rabbit visitors. It didn't take any time for the two to transform into the same fairies I'd spoken with the day before.

"Are all rabbits also fairies?" I asked before either of the tiny creatures could speak.

Vesta, with her pink skin and sassy attitude was the first to speak. "Doesn't she know anything?"

I took a sip of my coffee, fighting back the urge to tell her exactly where she could stick her attitude. Between the early morning hours, the lack of sleep, and still working on my first cup of caffeine, I wasn't in the mood to put up with her.

I didn't hear an answer, but she must have because she nodded and shrugged her shoulders looking off to my right as if someone was standing there.

Then again, maybe I was imagining things.

The two fairies began to hum in the same high pitched frequency so I couldn't make out what they were saying. From the body language of the two I guessed they were arguing. Again.

When they suddenly stopped fighting, they stared at the same spot behind me that Vesta had indicated to earlier. Glancing behind me, I couldn't see anything. Obviously, I needed more caffeine, so I took a long drink of my still-warm coffee, hoping it would wake me up and I'd stop thinking the fairies were talking to some invisible . . . something.

Then again, maybe I needed more than coffee.

"Would you two quit your arguing and answer my question," I finally demanded.

Both fae stared at me as if I were the one with wings growing out of my back.

Bill spoke first. "What question?"

"Are all rabbits also fairies?" I repeated.

"No," he replied. "But all fairies can be rabbits."

"Like that won't confuse her," came Vesta's snarky reply. She immediately looked as if she'd been scolded and I took a sip of my coffee to hide my juvenile pleasure at her discomfort, even if I didn't know the cause of that discomfort. I didn't think my smirk would help the situation at all, despite the ability to claim my rudeness on sleep deprivation.

I wasn't able to gloat long, however, before the two fairies resumed arguing in their native high-pitched tongue. For some reason I found the bickering more annoying than I had previously. And the pitch was grating on my nerves giving me a headache.

Finally, I couldn't take anymore. "If you two don't have anything to say to me, why don't you go back into the hills and leave me and my coffee in peace. Frankly, I'm too tired to listen to your nonsense."

Hotheaded Vesta began to shimmer, either in embarrassment or rage.

Bill, who had been more diplomatic the previous day, resumed that role. "Vesta," he hissed, glancing over my shoulder. "Mind your manners."

Before his reprimand set off another fit of arguing, I could smell the scent of well-worn leather. If my spirit guide was standing behind me, that would explain the fairies glances and best behavior.

"Look," I began, "I'm sure the two of you have other things to do today and I'm also sure that you don't want to be seen, right?" A dog barked in the distance as if punctuating my words.

Both fairies nodded their agreement.

"Then why don't you just tell me what you came to tell me and then you can get back to your . . . friends before the neighbors wake up."

Vesta regained her composure. "Fine. Here's what I know." She took a deep breath. "The dead guy wasn't from around here. In fact, he'd probably never even been here before. Like ever. The *dúnmhartóir*, though, he had been here before. Lots of times. Doesn't live around here, though."

I had no idea what *dúnmhartóir* meant and I had no intention of asking the feisty little fairy, but I guessed it meant murderer. The word had a Gaelic sound and I made a mental note to ask Mother about it next time we talked. Or maybe I'd try to find the word online. "Do you know where the. . ."

"*Dúnmhartóir?*" asked Vesta smugly when I struggled over the unfamiliar word.

"Yeah. Where's he—or she—from?"

"It's a he. And he's from LA."

"LA? Really? Are you positive?" Fairies could be tricky so I wanted to be sure.

Vesta rolled her eyes. "That's what I said, isn't it?"

Her answer made me almost giddy and I could feel tension slipping from my shoulders. If Joe could narrow down visitors with skull tattoos from Los Angeles, that would certainly help.

"Thank you," I exclaimed. "That's a huge help."

She gave me a smug smile, but didn't reply.

"Hey." Bill flew toward my face like an annoying mosquito. "I have something, too, you know."

"You do?" That both fae would have some information was more than I could have hoped for. "What did you learn?"

Bill stopped fluttering around and placed his hands upon his hips. "I thought you'd never ask." He cleared his throat before continuing. "Your dead guy, he had two lives."

"Two lives? What do you mean?"

"He has two pasts."

That confused me. "You mean like he led two separate lives? Two families or something?"

This time Bill rolled his eyes. "No. But his second life isn't the same as his first one."

I took another sip of my coffee, which had cooled off considerably, while I considered Bill's words. "Can you explain more?"

The fairy just shrugged.

He reminded me of Zach playing Twenty Questions with his sisters.

"Okay, can you tell me if the two lives coexist? Or did one follow the other?"

"One followed the other," Bill replied.

"Does anyone know about these two lives?"

"They were kept very separate."

"And his family didn't know about them?"

Bill didn't answer, but gave me a look that said *that's the stupidest question I've heard in a long time.*

"Would his wife know anything about that other life?"

"No."

I was at a loss. "Wait, does the murder have to do with one of those lives?"

A sly smile crept across Bill's face. "Yes," he said, wrinkling his nose just a little as he did.

This was getting more and more like Twenty Questions all the time. "Did his death have to do with his recent life?"

"No."

Well, that was something. "So the reason he was killed has to do with that first life?"

"Now you're getting it," Bill said.

In the distance someone yelled for a dog. A car door shut. Somewhere else a car started.

"We have to go." Vesta was respectful, yet forceful. "Before anyone comes around here."

While I understood their concern, I thought they had more to share. And I didn't want them to get out of helping that easily. "Is there anything else? Anything you can tell me?"

"Nope," Vesta announced as she began to shimmy and fade.

"His son." Bill's voice was tinged with sadness. "His son misses his dad. A lot."

I nodded. "That's understandable." And it was. I'd always been a "daddy's girl" and couldn't imagine losing my own father at this stage of my life, let alone as a young child.

Silently, I reflected on the child's loss when another idea struck me. "If Robert was killed for something in his distant past, how will Joe find the murderer?"

There was no answer. Rabbits were running away from the awakening neighborhood and I could no longer smell worn leather. The fairies—and He Who Waits—had left.

Chapter Twenty-One

It surprised me that I was a little disappointed He Who Waits hadn't said anything to me. Maybe I was getting the hang of this . . . whatever he was trying to teach me.

I didn't have long to ponder the situation, however, because I could hear the kids starting to move around inside the house. Why children are so difficult to get out of bed on a school day and such early risers any other day, I'd never know.

As I headed back into the house, Maddie met me in the kitchen. She still had sleep in her eyes and her long, blonde hair was a mess. "Who were you talking to, Mommy?"

"I wasn't talking to anyone, honey." Technically, that was true. Fairies and spirit guides didn't actually qualify as people since they weren't human.

"But I thought I heard you talking."

I didn't want to have a conversation about fairies and spirit guides with my husband, let alone my kids. As I was trying to decide what to tell her, the phone rang. "Why don't you make yourself some cereal?" I asked as I reached for the phone, silently thanking the universe for saving me from further inquisition by a sleepy six year old.

"Hello?" I watched Maddie pour the cereal and go to the refrigerator for some milk.

"What? No smart comment, Cerridwen?" Normally, I check the caller ID before answering. Junk calls, especially those recorded messages from various politicians, aggravate the saints and drive me crazy. However, since I've never been a morning person and I was so focused on not answering Maddie's questions, I hadn't bothered to look. When my mother's Irish lilt greeted me from the other end of the line, I remembered telemarketing companies didn't have a monopoly on badly timed phone calls.

Trying to make the best of the situation, I replied, "Not this morning, Ma. It's much too early."

Mother chuckled slightly. My loathing of mornings started long before I graduated from elementary school and had been a topic of contention between my naturally cheerful and alert mother and me.

I topped off my coffee cup as we chatted about the weather. I had the feeling Mother had something on her mind and wanted to make sure I was coherent enough to understand whatever she was about to say

Finally convinced that I could carry on a conversation, she got to the point. "You've been on my mind lately, lass."

Involuntarily, I rolled my eyes. "Well, I appreciate that, since you are my mother and all."

"Is everything okay there?" she continued, undaunted by my comment.

"Everything's fine, Ma. The kids are great, Matt's great, I'm great. No need to worry."

Her tsk was audible and conveyed her exasperation in a way words never could. "As a mother yourself, I would think you'd understand that I will always worry."

"I know, Ma." It was a lecture I'd heard numerous times in the past. "But we're all fine. Really."

Mother snorted like she had when I was a teen. "Maybe for now."

I took a deep breath and silently counted to ten. When she got an idea—especially one that involved her family's safety—my mother latched onto it with a tenacity that would make a pit bull jealous. When I reached ten I asked, "What do you think is the matter, Ma?"

"Well, now that you asked, I can't tell you. I just don't know."

That sounded a little nuts even for my mother.

When I didn't respond, she continued. "My darling Cerridwen, you've truly been on my mind the past few days. I honestly don't know why. I was hoping you could tell me."

"What?" for my entire life my mother *knew*. She knew if I were lying. She knew if I were in trouble. She just knew.

"I said," she began, annoyance making her Irish accent slightly more pronounced, "that I don't know why you've been on my mind. Honestly, lass, don't you pay attention?"

126

Even though she couldn't see me, I shook my head. "Ma, that's not what I meant."

She sighed. "I know, dear. I've been a bit of a curmudgeon the past few days and I haven't been sleeping well, besides." Mother sounded old, tired—attributes I had never heard from her before.

"Is everything okay, Ma? I mean, really okay?"

"Don't you be changing the subject, lass." Her voice regained its usual strength. "I didn't call to be talking about me, you know. I called about you."

That sounded more like my mother, but I made a mental note to call my sister later and find out what was going on. It was one of the rare moments when I regretted living hundreds of miles away from the rest of my family.

"Are you just going to sit and stew, or are you going to answer my question?"

"I'm sorry, Ma. Can you repeat that?"

She sighed. "I asked what was going on. Why do I get the impression you could be in danger, lass?"

I poured myself another cup of coffee and paced the kitchen as I quickly considered my words. "Dunno. Why don't you tell me what you think and maybe it will spark something?"

It was my mother's turn to stall. "Well, this will sound strange to you, I'm sure. But I dreamt you were a rowan tree."

She was right. That sounded strange, even for her. "A tree? You dreamt I was a tree?"

Ignoring me, she continued. "You were standing alone, a beautiful tree, such a deep green with a strong trunk. The berries still red, but as I looked more closely I saw that the leaves were starting to yellow and wither away, the berries weren't as fresh as I first thought. It seemed clear to me that the tree was dead, despite how healthy it looked at first glance."

"Really, Ma? You dreamt I was a dead tree?"

"Are you going to listen or are you going to mock?"

"Sorry, I'm listening." I took another sip of coffee and tried to pay attention.

"Thank you. So there you were standing alone atop a hillside when the sky began to darken. Dark storm clouds rolled in and I just knew there would be thunder and lightning not long after."

"Let me guess, lightning struck the tree."

"I'm not sure," Mother replied. "I woke up before the first rumbles of thunder."

My mother had been taking her dreams seriously since before I was born, so the fact she had a dream and believed there was some hidden message was nothing new. That she seemed so concerned by it was a little more disturbing. She couldn't have known about the odd thunderstorm over Bear Butte that was still fresh in mind. It made mother's dream seem a little creepy.

"Why would a dream like that make you think I was in danger," I asked, reluctant to admit anything. "And why would you think I was a tree?"

"I'm not sure why you were a tree, lass, other than to warn of the danger."

"You lost me again, Ma."

"It was the type of tree, Cerridwen." She clipped her words a tiny bit, a sure sign that she was starting to lose her patience.

"I know you told me, but what type of tree was it?"

"A rowan tree."

"What's so special about a rowan tree?" Besides fruit bearing trees—which even I could distinguish once the fruit started to grow—I knew pine trees, maple trees, and elm trees only if I studied the leaves and really thought about it. Rowans were a complete mystery. A mystery I had less desire to solve than the murder I'd been working on.

Mother sighed contently. "I thought you'd never ask, lass. Rowan trees are very special trees." She made "very special trees" sound like three separate sentences. "They have a great deal of significance."

I rolled my eyes but didn't respond.

She didn't seem to notice. "You see, lass, the rowan tree—a healthy one—has been a symbol of protection since the time of the druids. A rowan will take the negative energy and naturally transform it to something more positive."

"Oh-kay."

"Don't be so skeptical, Cerridwen."

"Sorry."

"The rowan's white flowers are a symbol of cleansing and safekeeping. Then, each of the berries hosts a tiny, five-pointed star at its base. Taken together, those are very powerful symbols."

I shook my head, knowing Mother couldn't see my reaction. The secret meaning of trees made my head want to explode.

"Stop shaking your head and rolling your eyes, Cerridwen. This is important."

I wasn't sure which was freaking me out more: that my mother and I were having a serious discussion about the meaning of trees or that even hundreds of miles away, she knew about the eye rolling and head shaking. Creepy advanced to a new level.

"Back to my dream and the trees," Mother continued, "and this time pay attention, lass. The rowan tree, as I've said, provides protection, but it's also a symbol of peace and of a connection to the Divine. But the tree in my dream wasn't a healthy tree. Its leaves were falling and the tree was dying."

"You mean like in the fall? When the season's change? You always told me that was just part of life. That things in nature— especially plants—were destined to die down and return later."

"Well, yes." She sounded apprehensive. "That's true. However, this was different."

"How do you mean?"

"Cerridwen, the tree was dead. Not hibernating—oh, that's not the right word, but you know what I mean."

"Actually, Ma, I think that is called hibernating, even in plants."

"Well, you learn something new every day, don't ya?"

"Ma. The tree?" Getting her back on track could be tricky if she strayed too far.

"Oh, yes. The tree. I mentioned the tree was truly dead, right?"

Although I couldn't stop the sigh from escaping, I tried to keep the annoyance out of my voice. "Yeah, Ma, you did."

"So if the tree were dead. . . ."

Not sure what type of response she was looking for, I asked,

"Would it matter how the tree died?"

"You know, lass, it might. But the idea of the tree *being* dead is important, also. It could mean that things are topsy-turvy." She was getting excited and her Irish accent became more pronounced as she spoke. "If that's the case, then, the rowan tree would be a warning that things are in upheaval, that there's no Divine connection, and that danger is lurking close by."

I almost expected a clap of thunder or ominous organ music to punctuate her words. Instead, a chorus of laughter came from the other room where the kids were watching cartoons. "Ma, what makes you think I'm the one in danger? It was your dream, after all. Maybe you're the one in danger. Or maybe sometimes a dream is just a dream."

"You are so like your father, aren't you? I realize that sometimes a dream is a dream and means nothing. This wasn't like that." As she spoke, my mother's voice began to remind me more and more of a college professor—passionate about the subject at hand, while trying to explain things slowly and methodically. I wondered when she had obtained that quality since I didn't remember her being that patient when I was growing up.

I tried to keep the sarcasm out of my voice. "Okay, Ma, let's say this dream wasn't really a dream and that it had something to do with me."

At that moment, a fight broke out in the other room. "Give that back!"

"No. I don't wanna watch that dumb show."

"I'm telling! Mmmmmoooommmmm!"

Based on the voices, all three children were wide awake and armed with their unique brand of sibling love. From the back of my mind I wondered who started it and what the easiest way to defuse the situation would be. All the commotion, however, meant I'd stopped paying attention to what my own mother was saying.

"So, lass, even if the face hadn't convinced me, the voice was definitely your's even if the words were not."

"Ma." The word came out more forcefully than I had intended and I made an effort to sooth my voice. "The kids are up and I can hear them fighting in the other room. Let me call you back later, okay? Love you, Ma."

Before she could say another word, I hung up the phone and went into peacekeeper mode as I headed toward the living room.

It wasn't until later that I realized I'd forgotten to ask her what *dúnmhartóir* meant.

Chapter Twenty-Two

I spent the next few hours refereeing one argument after another and the dynamics changed faster than I could mediate. I was tempted to send all three kids back to bed for the remainder of their summer vacation. Since that wasn't going to happen, I did the next best thing.

"They're all yours," I told Matt as he reached for a coffee cup, his hair sticking up on one end and pillow lines still marring his handsome face.

"Huh?"

"The fruit of your loins. They're yours and you may have them."

He filled his cup, took a sip, and groaned satisfyingly. "That bad already?"

I shrugged. "They're kids. They're siblings. They love each other. They drive each other nuts. And this morning, they've been driving me nuts, too."

He leaned over and kissed my cheek. "You didn't get much sleep either, did you?"

I shook my head.

"Feeling okay?"

"Just, I dunno, discombobulated or something."

"Because of the case? The one Agent Oliver asked you to help with?"

Another shrug. "Yeah, I guess so. It's hard to explain. Maybe I'm just really tired."

"Maybe." He didn't sound convinced. "Go back to bed. I'll take care of the Monster Trio for a few hours. Make sure they don't kill each other or anything."

I chuckled. "You'd have a lot of 'splaining to do," I said in my best Desi Arnaz voice, which sounded nothing like the Cuban celebrity.

Before I had a chance to say anything else, there was another commotion coming from the children. I sighed deeply, gritting my teeth as I did so.

"Go," Matt said. "I've got it. Get some rest."

I snatched the opportunity for retreat without another word. Instead of going back to bed, however, I headed for my office and the computer. I convinced myself I would just check my e-mails and complete the edits on an article about mothering twins I submitted to a national parenting magazine. I knew I was lying to myself and I wasn't doing a very good job of it, either.

The personal deception didn't stop me.

To ease my own conscious, I did check my e-mails. The edits took only a few moments. I stifled a yawn and rubbed my eyes. The computer screen seemed brighter than normal, another sure sign of impending exhaustion.

Since my brain seemed adverse to actually shutting down, I opened a web browser and typed "Los Angeles" into the search bar. I got breaking news and tourism sites, but nothing that would help find the killer. That would have been too easy.

I added words like "motorcycle," "biker," and "classic" and still got nothing more interesting than the distance from LA to the epicenter of the Black Hills Motorcycle Classic.

I sat starting at the screen with my elbows on the desk, my chin resting in my hands. My thoughts bounced around faster than a ping pong ball at the summer Olympics. Why would someone ride thirteen hundred miles from California to South Dakota to commit a murder? Did the dead guy have ties to California? Why was I having so much trouble thinking of him as "Robert" and not "the dead guy"? How come He Who Waits wasn't helping at all? Why were the kids being so quiet?

Mulling over what little I knew wasn't getting me anywhere, either. I sat up straight and placed my fingers on the keyboard's "home row," before typing "Robert Mesmer" into the search engine. This time I got something pertinent—a web site mentioning his insurance business. A few more keystrokes led me to the insurance company's site and a professionally taken picture of the deceased. In his long-sleeved, button-down, shirt and power-red tie, he didn't look like the bikers I'd seen during my excursion to the classic.

He Who Waits had said something about things not always being what they seem. Maybe he was talking about the bikers. If one—

well, two if I counted the undercover agent—hid things, then it stood to reason that others did, too.

"So what are you hiding, Robert Mesmer?" I asked aloud.

After reading his brief biography on the company web site, I hit the back button and resumed my search. I found what was probably his home address and phone number on one site and some pictures on a social networking site. Other than that, I didn't know any more than I did before. And none of it was probably going to help find the killer. Anything I'd found online had surely been found and thoroughly investigated by the professionals. That's what made them professionals. It stood to reason that whatever resources the FBI had were surely better than my home computer.

Undaunted, I kept searching, still not learning anything new about Robert or his life outside the insurance company. I also couldn't find much about Robert's childhood, but I didn't dwell on that. There probably weren't many online pictures of me as a child, either. Although, anyone who really wanted to could probably find something about my childhood, if they only knew where to search.

Where to search? That was the question. There had to be something—anything—about Robert's life outside the insurance company.

My thoughts continued in this circle making my head start to throb. I put my elbows on the desk and started rubbing my forehead.

"Start with what you know." He Who Wait's voice penetrated my thoughts.

I didn't remember the spirit guide using those words, and he didn't seem to be in the room with me since I couldn't smell the leather scent I associated with his presence, however the advice seemed like something he would dole out.

"What I know," I mumbled. "What do I know? Nothing."

I sat up straight and rolled my head around, trying to loosen the muscles that were tightening in my neck and back before I reached for the computer and returned to the insurance company's site. A few more clicks and I had returned to Robert's biography. I read it more closely this time, looking for any clue to what may have played a part in his death.

A line I missed the first time stood out as if it had been flashing in ten-foot tall neon letters.

"Robert and his wife, Ellen, are valued members of Perkins Insurance Company."

His wife, Ellen.

I was only a few clicks away from Ellen's biography. It didn't have much more personal information then Robert's but it did list her professional name as Ellen Perkins Mesmer. Another web search, this time for Ellen Perkins Mesmer, got me to a popular social media site. On that site I found pictures of not only Ellen, but also Robert and a young child I assumed to be their son. I was a little surprised that the page wasn't only available to friends, but that didn't stop me from skimming through the information.

Feeling a little like a peeping tom, I glanced through the posts on the page. Older ones had famous quotes or short updates on her day: things like "great time at the lake" or "not looking forward to work after the great weekend." More recently, however, the page was filled with messages of thoughts and prayers and condolences. Reading them made me feel even more like I was prying into Ellen's personal life.

A wave of sadness and regret washed over me. Sadness for the survivors and regret for a life cut short. Even though I was sure I wouldn't find anything that would help, I went back to Ellen's pictures, hoping I'd see something that would spark something. At least that's what I told myself. What I really wanted was to see a time when the family was happy, before tragedy struck.

An album entitled "family" seemed promising, so I started there. Pictures of various holidays and birthdays were sprinkled among candid shots of friends and family. Many of the photos prominently featured a young boy, often with Ellen. Reading the captions, told me it was the couple's son and waves of regret returned. I couldn't stop myself from looking at the photos and getting lost in the knowledge that this family had been changed forever.

Somewhere between my overwhelming melancholy and the adorable pictures on the site, I completely lost track of time. The familiar *ping* of an instant message brought me out my fog. "Talk to

135

Ma lately?" my sister typed.

"She called this morning," I replied, resisting the urge to highlight the word *called*. As a 9-1-1 dispatcher, Wendy didn't spend any extra time on the phone. Ever.

"So she told you about her dream, right?"

"She told you? I thought the dream was about me."

"Ma just wanted a second opinion. She knew you'd be adverse to the message and needed a sympathetic ear first. "

For a moment I was grateful that we were IMing, that way Wendy couldn't tell how frustrated I was. "I listened."

"Did it make sense to you? Was Ma's message something you needed to hear?"

"I guess." It didn't make sense, but I hoped Wendy would take my word for it. I wasn't in the mood to have my younger sister lecture me on the ways of the Universe.

"Good," she typed. "Cuz sometimes people just don't recognize the clues when they see them."

"True." It seemed like an odd thing for her say, but it did make sense.

When Wendy didn't respond right away, I returned to Ellen's photo album. I wasn't really paying attention to the pictures I was looking at, but I couldn't stop my inner voyeur, either. I was a few pictures into the album and my mind was wandering when something made me stop. I saw something. I was sure of it.

The photo I was stopped at didn't seem special: the child was posing with an oversized baseball bat. I went back a photo—one of the kid making a funny face—and didn't see anything important there, either. I clicked back one more photo when I noticed something.

A tattoo.

Of a decorative skull.

Chapter Twenty-Three

Quickly, I went back through as many of Ellen's pictures as I could and not just in the "family" album. This time I wasn't meandering aimlessly through someone else's memories. I was looking for pictures of Robert, hoping to see another image of his tattoo.

I didn't see one. In fact, there were few images of Robert to start with and he sported long sleeves in almost all of them.

After scrutinizing the one photo where I thought I saw the skull tattoo, I began to wonder if I was imagining things. Maybe what looked like a tattoo was really a weird shadow. Or maybe it was a temporary tattoo. Or maybe it *was* a skull tattoo and meant absolutely nothing.

My eyes had started to hurt and my neck felt sore from staring at the computer screen for so long. A hot shower would do wonders for my aching muscles and the change of venue might even clear my head.

It didn't. Instead I found myself obsessing over the last time the bathroom had been thoroughly scrubbed. As if obsessing over a clean bathtub was any better than obsessing over a murder. At least I could control the state of the bathroom.

I had barely dressed from my shower when the phone rang. At least I thought the phone rang, since with the towel covering my wet hair also covered my ears and muffled any sound that managed to make it's way into the still steamy bathroom.

All doubts were alleviated with a faint rap on the door.

"Mommy, you have a phone call," Maddie announced as she opened the door. I was going to have to remind her to wait until she was told it was okay before opening doors. At least she'd remembered to knock this time and that was a step in the right direction.

She held the cordless phone toward me as if it were a special prize.

"Hello?" I shooed Maddie away and shoved the towel up over my ear, trying to keep the bulk of my wet curls from escaping.

"Cerri, I'm sorry," came Joe's voice, a cross between authoritative and apologetic. "I told her not to bother you."

That explained Maddie's lack of chatter into the phone and even the reverence she displayed in handing it to me. Both girls had developed a crush on the handsome FBI agent.

"It's okay," I began. "I'm actually glad you called. I have some information for you." I think, I added silently.

"I'm glad." I heard the relief seep into his voice. "Whatcha got?"

Without telling him how I learned anything, I relayed the information the fairies had told me and even mentioned that I'd found pictures of Robert on his wife's social media pages. That confession caused Joe to chuckle on the other end of the line.

"What's so funny? Did you already know all this?" The idea that I had to pay a bunch of fairies—two bunches of fairies—for information Joe already had irritated me beyond belief and I was ready to hang up and add his number to our blocked calls list. Or maybe the lack of sleep was catching up again.

Joe cleared his throat, probably trying to stop himself from laughing. "I was just thinking that you would make a good investigator, Cerri."

His compliment was probably backhanded, but it did squelch my frustration. A little. "Thanks," I mumbled. "But you knew all that didn't you?"

"Actually, we knew about the insurance company," he began. "But nothing about California, so that's a new direction to look in. The reason I called, though, is that I have some files that I'd like you to take a look at. I'll be there in about ten minutes."

I didn't have time to protest before the line went dead.

Chapter Twenty-Four

The ten minutes I'd been afforded barely left me any time to warn Matt and the kids, let alone get dressed. At least I'd already showered.

The next item on my agenda was straightening the living room where my three monsters had made themselves comfortable while watching television. A blanket here, an empty bowl there. My goal was to make sure the room could be walked through, even if it would never grace the cover of an interior design magazine.

In the few minutes before our uninvited guest was due to arrive, Maddie and Kenzie each found time to dress and comb their hair. Zach, on the other hand, had to be coaxed out of his pajamas. I'm pretty sure Matt bribed him with the promise of looking at dirt bikes. I wanted to scold my husband, but opted to count my blessings that he didn't mention the puppy to the girls.

Besides, just as I opened my mouth to say something, the doorbell rang.

"I'll get it," came a chorus of six-year-old voices as the girls ran toward the front door.

"Freeze." Matt's voice echoed as he spoke and I had no trouble imagining him in front of a lecture hall where he would conduct classes. "*I* will answer the door," he said more softly, yet still not leaving any room for discussion. "You two go play or go watch TV. The grownups have to talk."

The disappointment on the twins faces was matched only by the smugness on their brother's. His reprimand involved no words, only the look Matt gave his son. Zach quietly followed his sisters, sulking.

From my vantage point between the hall and the living room I watched the scene unfold, leaning against the door jam, with my arms crossed over my chest. Judging by the look on Zach's face, I figured he must not want to take any chances with the promise of a motocross bike to be so accommodating. Maybe I'd have to rethink my stance on the bike.

Nah. They were still two-wheeled death traps and putting my son atop one was asking to go into debt to the nearest orthopedic surgeon since broken limbs were the least lethal of all possible outcomes.

I shook my head in an effort to drive the offending thoughts from my mind. It didn't work, especially when Joe's presence reminded me of the recent violence at Bear Butte. If a grown man on vacation wasn't safe, what would make anyone think a child on a dirt bike would be? It didn't really matter that the two events weren't related in the least.

". . . and should be landing soon." Joe's voice brought be back to the present. He and Matt had taken seats in the living room and were both looking at me expectantly, but I had no idea why.

"What do you think, Cerri? Do you want to meet the widow?" Matt asked. "I can handle the kids. You might be of some comfort to her."

I could have kissed him for coming to my rescue like that. "If you think it will help."

Both men shrugged, but it was Joe who spoke. "I don't see how it could hurt. Maybe you'll notice something we don't. Or maybe she'll open up to you. You not being law enforcement might encourage her to open up even more. Besides, women feel more comfortable with other women during an emotional situation, right?"

Personally, my preferred method of dealing with highly emotional situations involved chocolate and ice cream. Often together, but not always. To Joe, I directed a non-committal grunt. Or at least what I hoped was a non-committal grunt.

Matt motioned for me to sit down and I ambled my way toward him.

"What's it gonna hurt?" my husband whispered as I sat beside him.

It was my turn to shrug.

"Is that a yes?" Joe sounded both relieved and hopeful. As if he knew I'd eventually agree.

Matt answered. "I told you she'd help. Cerri has a heart of gold."

I felt myself blush at the compliment and squeezed Matt's hand in silent thanks. "Enough flattery." Turning to Joe I continued, "Let's get going."

No sooner had the words left my mouth than the kids were back in the living room with cries of wanting to go with us. It annoyed me more than nails on a chalkboard and I was angry with myself for my temperament. Maybe a time out would have done me some good, but I didn't foresee that happening anytime soon.

I didn't know why things were getting on my nerves so badly, and I knew I didn't have the time to analyze my attitude, so I plastered a smile on my face, reminded the kids that we needed to go, and headed for the door. Matt grabbed my hand and kissed me on the cheek. "Be careful," he whispered in my ear. "Remember, I love you."

Hearing those words helped my attitude more than a king-size chocolate bar. I twisted my head enough to give him a kiss on the cheek. "I love you, too."

Once Joe and I had made it out the door, I was startled to hear his chuckle.

"What are you laughing at?" I asked as I climbed into his vehicle.

He didn't answer until he was buckled into the driver's seat. "You. Your family. It's cute."

This side of the FBI Agent was one I had never seen and, frankly, didn't know how to respond to. Raising my eyebrow at him in uncertainty, I remained quiet.

Neither of us spoke again until we were closer to Rapid City. That's when I broke the silence, finally voicing the thing that had been eating away at me since we'd left my house. "What if. . .what if I can't get anything? Anything helpful, I mean."

Joe shrugged, never taking his eyes from the road. "Then you don't. We do have some leads, you know. I guess I was just hoping that you knew something we didn't."

Loathe to admit that I knew nothing, I changed the subject. "Why do you want me to meet Ellen?"

A wry smile crossed Joe's face. "You're the body language expert, right?"

He had been told that when we worked together before. Other than a few internet articles and years of conducting interviews as a journalist, however, I didn't have any clue as to what a person's body language actually meant. Joe's FBI training probably made him more qualified to read people.

Thankfully, he didn't wait for me to respond. "Like I said earlier, maybe you'll pick up on something. Maybe the wife will talk to you more than she will me or another agent."

We were stopped at a stoplight, waiting to turn onto Highway 44 toward the airport.

"I guess," I said, not knowing how else to respond.

"You'll be fine. I know you will." The light had changed and Joe was headed east toward the airport. "Hell, I appreciate any help you can give me. I hate having to talk with the families left behind."

Even though he didn't expand, something about the way Joe said those words made me think the FBI Agent had experience delivering the news, as well as receiving it and it made me wonder about his personal life.

I stared out the window, noticing my reflection more than the scenery, remembering the last time I traveled this far east on Highway 44. That time I was driving and had a gun pointed at me. The memory was still raw, but kept asserting itself no matter how hard I tried to repress it. The shiver that ran down my spine had more to do with the memory then it did the air conditioning blasting from the car's vents.

"Are you—" Joe didn't finish. Instead, he slammed on the brakes, just as a motorcycle cut in front of us. The car fishtailed just a little, and I felt my own muscles tighten in response to the action.

The offending driver continued on, seemingly oblivious to the accident that almost was.

Beside me, Joe let out a deep breath. "You okay?"

I was shaking with the possibility of what could have happened. Aloud I replied, "Yep. I'm good. You?"

"It's a good thing I was paying attention. No indicator at all."

"There's never a cop around when you want one," I said before I could think the words through. I could feel my face reddening as I realized how the FBI Agent may take those words.

I needn't have worried.

"Nope, never is," Joe responded, a hint of humor peppering his words and causing the corners of his mouth to turn up, but not quite making it all the way to his eyes.

We spent the remainder of the ride making small talk, with him asking most of the questions and me providing the answers. I didn't mind; he had asked about a topic I was passionate about—my children. Most of the conversation covered things he already knew or could guess; their ages, grades in school, and their individual likes and dislikes.

"All three of the kids enjoy a good story, but Mackenzie is turning out to be the biggest reader. Madison is more hands-on. I think it's harder for her to sit still, even. Zach, well, Matt describes Zach as 'all boy.' I guess that's accurate. He's much more of a daredevil than either of his sisters." I shrugged. "I don't have any brothers, so I don't know."

Joe nodded as he pulled into the airport's parking lot. "I was always doing more dangerous things than my sisters were."

"You have sisters?" It was the first time Joe had mentioned anything about his personal life and I was more than a little amazed that he chose to confide even that much to me.

"Three. One older, two younger." His eyes relaxed, as if he were recalling the adventures of his youth. "I would do things to annoy my older sister and then threaten my younger ones to not do whatever I did."

I chuckled, thinking of the warnings I'd overheard my son give his sisters. "That sounds like Zach. And now he wants a motocross bike. Can you imagine it?"

By this time we had parked and were getting out of the car. I noticed Joe smiling as he replied, "The daredevil stage. I remember it well."

"How long does it last?" My words were more optimistic than my voice, which cracked with fear as I spoke.

Joe answered as he stepped into the airport's revolving door. "I'll let you know when I outgrow mine."

Chapter Twenty-Five

His words hit me like a punch in the stomach as I followed him through the revolving doors and into the airport. "You mean you never got out of that daredevil phase?" I asked when I'd caught up to Joe, who had stopped to check the electronic board announcing the arrivals and departures.

"Nope. One of the reasons I became an FBI agent. Always something different. No two days alike." He glanced my direction. "Come on. Her flight's arrived. We'll probably find her at the baggage claim."

With two runways and a handful of gates, Rapid City's airport wasn't big. The ticket counter was to our right and the conveyer belt signaling the baggage claim area was to the left. It would have been hard to miss, even without the groan of the machine as it awoke.

Coming down the stairs and escalator were a multitude of people who I assumed had just landed. I tried to be nonchalant as I searched faces for the Ellen Mesmer I remembered from the web site. Nonchalant, however, had never been one of my strong points and more than one passerby gave me the evil eye for staring.

Joe wasn't much better. He was assessing every woman who passed by. Whether it was his air of authority, the fact he was an attractive man, or that he'd had more practice at the art of nonchalant, I noticed he received far fewer glares. The difference was so incredible that I finally quit looking at the crowd and began to find my hands overly fascinating while wondering how long this would take and how I'd managed to get involved with another police investigation.

Still lost in my own thoughts, I didn't notice when Ellen first appeared and, had Joe not nudged my elbow, I possibly could have missed her altogether. The polished, professional woman from the web site was gone and had been for some time, if the two inches of dark roots pushing at her otherwise straw-colored hair was any indication. I glanced at her hands where her once claw-like nails had

144

missed more than one appointment with her manicurist. I could empathize with her recent loss, but the chipped nails polish and excessive roots hinted that she had neglected her overall appearance for some time.

Or maybe I was being overly critical. The woman did just lose her husband, after all.

While I was being snarky, Joe had approached the widow and pulled her aside and began to lead her off to a more secluded area of the open room. He motioned for me to join them, so I meandered toward them, still not knowing exactly why the FBI agent wanted me there.

". . .for your loss, and I know you've spoken with my colleges out in Washington State, however, I do have a few more questions for you."

She sniffled. "Oh, well, okay." Her voice was high pitched and still had the tell-tale rasp of someone who'd been crying. "But not here. I can't do it here."

"No, ma'am. We'd like to go somewhere a little more private. Perhaps our offices? I'm sure this is a very difficult time for you."

She sniffed again. "It is." Ellen glanced once in my direction before continuing. "May I get my bags first?"

"Of course," Joe replied, leading the widow toward the now almost-empty baggage area. "Did you have someone meeting you?"

She shook her head, but remained silent.

"A rental car set up?"

Ellen shook her head again. "I didn't think of that." She sounded defeated.

Joe took a deep breath and scrunched his brow as if in thought. "Why don't you and Cerri go get your luggage, and I'll have a car delivered to our offices? Then we can get this over as quickly as possible."

His suggestion was met with a nod.

As he headed toward the car rental counter on the far left side of the building, Ellen and I slowly fought the wave of travelers and made our way to the baggage carousel. A naturally private person, I had no idea what to say to this stranger who was obviously hurting.

Thankfully, Ellen spoke first.

"So, what's it like to be in the FBI?"

"Um, well, I'm not. Not in the FBI, I mean."

The pink creeping into her cheeks spoke of embarrassment. "Oh, I just assumed. Because he said . . . ." She indicated toward Joe, who was still at the car rental counter.

"Not a problem." I wanted to put her at ease and remembered why Joe said he wanted me to tag along. "I work with Agent Oliver sometimes. He thought you might feel more comfortable with a woman present." It made me feel better to know that at least I didn't lie.

Ellen nodded, but didn't say anything. She rubbed her eyes before wiping her nose with the back of her hand. I knew better than to search my purse for a tissue. Bandages, I could have provided, but tissues were lacking.

As I wondered what to say that might comfort the woman, she spoke. "I guess I should get my suitcase, shouldn't I?" Her voice cracked and her eyebrows rose just a little as if she were asking my permission. It was another way meeting her in person contrasted with the well-put-together image I'd formed based on the web site and I reminded myself again that everyone deals with grief differently.

We walked toward the massive conveyor belt. The area had thinned out a lot and only a handful of people were still waiting for their own bags. One piece of expensive-looking luggage was headed back into the abyss. A matching piece was three feet behind.

Ellen pointed to the piece still visible on the conveyor. "That's mine." Her brow winkled as if she were confused. "But there's another one, too."

"Matching?"

She nodded.

"It just went to the back. It should be right out." I felt like I was trying to explain something to one of my kids and wondered if Ellen Mesmer was going to be alright.

Ellen and I collected her luggage, which wasn't as heavy as I had anticipated, and made our way toward the car rental counter where Joe stood waiting.

"They'll deliver the car to our offices downtown," he said as we approached.

Ellen nodded, but said nothing.

Joe took the suitcase Ellen was holding and led us toward his car. After depositing the luggage in the truck, Joe offered Ellen the front seat. I climbed into the back.

As I did so, I heard Ellen sniffle again. It also sounded like she stifled a sob and it reminded me of He Who Wait's telling me that all cultures honor their dead. If cultures all honored their ancestors differently, it stood to reason that individual people had to grieve differently.

When another sniffle accompanied the start of the engine, I thought of my own life. I pictured my mother as a widow and knew that, while she would miss my dad immensely, her married life had been made up of smaller separations while my dad served in the military. Being apart was something they could handle—not necessarily like, but handle. On the other hand, I barely tolerated the few months Matt and I had to be apart when we moved to the Black Hills. I couldn't imagine losing him forever. I knew I'd be a basket case if something were to happen to him.

My heart went out to the young widow sitting in front of me.

Chapter Twenty-Six

The drive to the FBI field office was eerily quiet. Only Ellen broke the silence with her sniffles and muffled sobs. Every time I heard her sounds of grief, my heart broke a little more. By the time we reached Rapid City's limits, I wanted to scoop the widowed woman into my arms encourage her to cry it out.

Instead, I picked at my fingernails until Joe parked outside the Federal Building. It wasn't productive, but I didn't know what else to do from the backseat of the vehicle.

We arrived at the Federal Building and Joe led the way to the FBI offices. None of us spoke and Ellen's sniffles echoed though the institutional corridor.

Joe led us to an interview room and motioned toward the uncomfortable looking chairs surrounding a metal table.

"I'll be right back," he announced. "Can I get either of you something to drink? Coffee? Water?"

I shook my head, but Ellen mumbled that water would be fine.

Neither of us spoke until Joe returned. I still had no idea what to say to this grieving woman I'd just met. The silence gave me the opportunity to look around the room. It reminded me of every interview room I'd seen on the various crime dramas I liked watching. Only this one wasn't as nice.

When Joe returned, he brought Ellen's water and a notepad. Still no one spoke until he took a seat.

Joe's deep breath and Ellen's sob were simultaneous. It struck me that both of them were trying to prepare for the task, but only one would leave the room with any answers. Ellen could tell Joe everything about her late husband, but the FBI Agent wasn't going to be able to answer the one question foremost on Ellen's mind. Who killed Robert?

Joe spoke first. "Mrs. Mesmer, I am very sorry for your loss."

Ellen nodded and daubed at her eyes, but didn't speak.

Joe looked miserable and I felt as sorry for him as I did her. He glanced at me, his eyes pleading for help.

Not knowing what he expected of me, I spoke the words I'd been thinking since we'd left the airport. "I can't imagine what you're going through."

Ellen took a deep, ragged breath, clenching her eyes tightly as she exhaled.

"Tell me about your husband," I prompted. "Tell me about Robert."

Her face lit up, but her eyes maintained the grief that I imagined would be a part of her life for eternity. "Rob is—was—nothing more than a big teddy bear. He would do anything for Chase and me. He'd give us the moon, if he could. Chase—that's our son—he doesn't understand why daddy isn't coming home."

She paused and took another ragged breath, as if trying to steady her nerves. I reached over and patted her hand, hoping the human contact would give her strength. With her other hand, Ellen wiped at her eyes. Tears remained at bay, but threatened to overflow at any moment.

"It's okay," I said softly. "Take your time."

"I didn't think it would be so hard," Ellen said. She took a sip of water before continuing. Somewhere I'd heard that sipping water would keep a person from crying and I wondered if Ellen was going to prove or disprove the statement. "Rob wasn't perfect. But he was a good man. He…he barely ever raised his voice, he would rather spend time with Chase and me than go out with his friends, he would even make me breakfast in bed on Saturdays. Like I said, he was a good man. I can't believe he's gone. I…I thought we'd grow old together."

There was a moment of silence before I spoke again, hoping Joe wouldn't mind me asking so many questions. "You also worked together, right?"

Ellen nodded as she sniffled again. "Yeah. The company was started by my dad. I got my license a few months before Rob did. Dad hired him right away. Rob knew just about everything about vehicles. And he was meticulous with his paperwork. He could put anyone at ease. He was so giving. I can't believe this has happened."

Joe spoke. "Did he have any trouble at work? Clients? Co-workers?"

Ellen shook her head. "There's no co-workers except me and Caroline. My dad doesn't even do more than sign the paychecks."

"Who's Caroline?" Joe asked.

Ellen looked surprised, but I wasn't sure if her shock came from the question or that Joe asked it. "Um, Caroline Bowers. She's our receptionist."

Joe nodded as he wrote something down. "What about clients?"

"What about them?" Ellen asked.

"Did Rob have problems with any of his clients?"

Ellen shook her head twice before stopping as if frozen. "Wait. There was one man who threatened Rob a month or so ago." Her eyes went wide as she turned toward me. "You don't think Mr. Harrison killed Rob, do you?"

I didn't know what to say and could almost feel Ellen's panic take root.

Thankfully, Joe knew how to respond. "Mrs. Mesmer, we're just trying to determine exactly what happened. Who's Mr. Harrison?"

"Dennis Harrison is a grumpy, old man," Ellen said. "He's in his late 60s or early 70s. We've been his insurance agents for years. He was one of my dad's first clients. I think I've known him my whole life."

"Why do you call him a grumpy, old man?" I asked.

"He's been a grumpy, old man for as long as I've known him. Always complaining. It's too hot, it's too cold. It's too wet, it's too dry. He always finds something to complain about." Ellen's sorrowfulness lifted for a brief moment before she spoke again. "Rob used to say that Mr. Harrison wasn't happy unless he was complaining, and even then he would be upset because no one else was complaining."

"Why would Mr. Harrison have threatened Rob?"

"Um, there was some kind of problem with his claim. I don't remember all the details, but Rob didn't recommend paying it. He thought there was some kind of fraud. Mr. Harrison had shown up with his son-in-law and Rob told them there were some

150

inconstancies. Mr. Harrison blew up."

"Do you remember what kind of claim it was?" Joe asked. "Home? Auto?"

"Home, I think. Caroline could fax you the file, I'm sure. Everything would be in it. Like I said, Rob is…was meticulous about policies."

Joe nodded, but I spoke. "Mr. Harrison was in his late 60s, you said? What did he say to Rob to threaten him?"

Tears began to well up again in Ellen's eyes. "Mr. Harrison started yelling that Rob was cheating him and defaming his character and that if Rob didn't take it back, Mr. Harrison would make him pay. That he'd be sorry."

To me it sounded a lot like an older man with a short temper who used intimidation as a style of argument. "But Mr. Harrison didn't get more specific?"

Ellen shook her head before verifying my impressions. "I've known Dennis Harrison most of my life. He's a jerk and a loud mouth, but that's it. You know, all bark and no bite?"

"What about his son-in-law?" Joe asked. "You mentioned that the son-in-law was there, also."

She nodded and sniffled at the same time. "Right. Gabe Kessler. Rob didn't mention him saying much."

"Would Rob have made a note of anything Gabe said? In that file you mentioned?" Joe's voice had resumed the professional quality I was more accustomed to and lost some of the compassion that had been there. The change made me assume he'd heard something that attracted his cop radar.

Ellen seemed not to notice the change in the FBI Agent's tone as she squeezed her eyes shut as if she were again fighting back tears. "I'm sure he would have," she almost whispered.

Joe nodded once and, when he spoke again, his voice had lost some of the cold edge he'd previously used. "Tell me about Gabe Kessler."

"He's a quiet version of his father-in-law. He doesn't get loud, but I don't think he's ever happy with anything. I always felt sorry for Marie—that's his wife—for having to deal with such miserable men her entire life."

"Did you hear Gabe threaten your husband?"

Ellen shook her head. "I didn't hear anything. Like I said, Gabe's real quiet. Besides, he left right after that meeting for Sydney Lake, Ontario. A bunch of guys go up there and go fishing every year."

I found Ellen's recollection of the day interesting, but wasn't sure how any of it was helpful to finding Robert's killer. I took a deep breath and was disappointed when the smell of leather eluded me. If He Who Waits would show up, maybe I could figure out what I was missing or even if talking with Ellen was going to help. I had serious doubts.

"And Gabe was leaving right then? Are you sure?"

Ellen nodded. "It's always the same time every year. Down to the same hour. Besides, Gabe's fishing poles were in the car. I saw them. Through the windshield."

She looked down as she spoke, giving the impression that she wasn't telling us everything. Again I wished He Who Waits would show up and offer some insight.

"… didn't go?" Joe asked Ellen something while I was lost in my own thoughts.

"We had a fight." Ellen's voice cracked and silent tears rolled down her cheeks. "That was the last face-to-face conversation we had."

Chapter Twenty-Seven

I reached across the interview table and touched Ellen's hand, wondering what they'd fought about. It seemed too personal to ask, but I knew from experience that Joe probably thought the petite widow a suspect. The FBI Agent seemed to think everyone was a suspect until he could prove they weren't. I didn't think she had anything to do with her husband's death, but my information wasn't concrete proof, either.

Before Joe could speak, I began, "Oh, I'm so sorry. I can't imagine what you're going through. I hate to ask, but what did you fight about?"

"Money. Work. Clients," Ellen said, tears still rolling down her face. "I thought he was too harsh with Dennis and Gabe. I mean, I know they weren't exactly friends, but . . . . Anyway, that's what it started as, what set me off. But there was more."

I understood that. More than once in my own married life I'd argued with Matt over something minor when really it was something else actually bothering me. Sometimes I couldn't even put a finger on exactly what that "something else" was.

As sexist as it may be, I suspected Joe would have no idea what Ellen had meant. A quick glance at Joe confirmed my suspicions. Turning my attention back to Ellen, I asked, "Had you two been having problems?"

Ellen shrugged. "It seems so stupid now. But, yes. Well, not really. I thought . . . I thought he was seeing someone else."

I tried not to let my shock show, but I could feel my eyes widen in surprise. An affair would be enough to put Matt's life in danger. While I was searching my brain to find a tactful way to get more information out of Ellen, Joe jumped in.

"Why would you think that, Mrs. Mesmer?"

Ellen looked toward the ceiling, as her lip began to quiver. "Please don't misunderstand me. I love my husband. I do. And he is—was a good man." She drew in a ragged breath. "But he wasn't perfect and he wasn't always easy to live with."

I nodded. "Go on."

"Rob never talked about his childhood. Ever. Not once did I hear him mention his parents or his grade school or the name of a friend. At first, that didn't matter to me. But after Chase was born, I wanted his parents to know their grandchild. I'm not proud of it, but I began nagging him."

I didn't need any help from the spirit world to know how that scenario played out. "And he got more secretive and more defensive, didn't he?"

Ellen nodded. "So I got more, I dunno, obnoxious. I started checking his cell phone records."

"What did you find?" Joe asked.

"Long distance calls once a month. And it wasn't an area code that I knew. I don't remember the number, but they were never more than a minute. Literally." Ellen's laugh was more sad than humorous. "I even tried calling a friend for that amount of time and there wasn't time for more than a 'hello' on her end. And that number never called his phone. He always called."

"Did you ask him about it?" If it had been me, I'd have asked Matt. Loudly. Often. And his answer had better be good.

"I did. Rob told me to mind my own business. He'd never spoken to me like that before. Ever. I thought about it a long time. And I decided that he was entitled to his privacy about those calls. I mean, the calls were so short…"

That sounded crazy. "You what?"

Ellen looked at me, her cheeks still wet with tears. "Rob was a good man. But it was like whatever happened before we met, he wanted to forget. To pretend it didn't exist. I decided arguing about a few thirty-second calls wasn't worth it."

Joe continued the questioning. "And you never found out who they were to?"

Ellen shook her head. "Not really. I asked Rob's uncle about the number once. He said he didn't know who Rob would be calling, but I could tell he was lying. He knew who it was. Then I overheard the two of them arguing about it later. I figured Rob would tell me eventually. Now he never will."

"Was this recently, Mrs. Mesmer?"

"No. This was maybe a year or two ago."

Now I was confused. "And you still thought he was having an affair?"

"A few months after that, the calls ended," Ellen explained. "I tried to ask Rob about it, but he wouldn't say anything. It drove me crazy, but the calls had stopped. Rob started to lighten up a little. Laugh more. Then a month or so ago, he got very secretive again. Like I said, he never did talk about his childhood or much about anything before we met, but it was like he got, I don't know, depressed or unhappy or something. I wondered if maybe he'd found someone else. Maybe he was growing tired of me. Of our life together."

The smell of leather filled the room, but no one else seemed to react. He Who Waits appeared in the corner. "He found no one."

Not thinking, I opened my mouth to respond when I suddenly remembered no one else in the room could see or hear my spirit guide. I tried to play it cool, but I probably looked like a fish out of water snapping my mouth back shut as quickly as I did.

The quizzical glance from Joe told me I failed at "looking cool."

Quickly, I tried another route. "But he wasn't having an affair, was he?" As I asked the question, He Who Waits vanished.

In response to my question, Ellen again shook her head. "I don't think so. Look, I know it probably sounds crazy to you. It sounds crazy to me. But for all his faults, Rob never lied. Even about his past. He just wouldn't answer. But he never lied."

It was a safe guess that Joe wasn't believing that.

"What happened a month ago?" I asked.

"His uncle died. Heart attack. Rob was devastated."

I had a good idea how that played out. "He shut you out again, didn't he?"

Ellen nodded, but didn't speak. The tears which had previously subsided were again threatening to escape down her cheeks and I wondered how I would hold up in her position. I didn't want to ever find out. Aloud, I asked, "You never really thought he was having an affair, did you?"

155

She sniffled. "Not really. I just didn't know what else to blame. I don't know why he would shut down like that, why he wouldn't tell me what was wrong. I thought either he found someone else or it was me. I just don't know. Maybe he just didn't love me anymore."

Her last few words were almost unintelligible due to her sobs. I glanced at Joe as he opened his mouth. Shaking my head slightly, hoping he would understand that Ellen needed more time to compose herself. Besides, she hadn't killed her husband and probably didn't know anything more.

Joe must have understood what I was trying to convey, because he nodded once before motioning toward the door.

I asked Ellen if she minded if we left for a few minutes. It probably wasn't the way Joe would have done it, but he seemed to have let me run this interview. Ellen indicated that it wasn't a problem and we left her with her tears.

Joe shut the door once we reached the hallway. "She doesn't know anything."

"No, I don't think she does," I agreed.

"And I know she didn't actually kill her husband," Joe replied, leaning against the wall.

"You didn't actually think she did, did you?"

He shrugged. "Everyone's a suspect, remember? And it's usually someone close to the victim."

"Well, Ellen didn't do it," I said more forcefully than I meant to.

Joe chuckled. "Relax. I know that. But now I also know that she didn't hire someone to do it, either."

"You thought she could have?"

"It was a possibility."

I weighed my next words carefully. "Robert wasn't having an affair."

Joe's eyebrow raised, but he said nothing.

I continued. "So whatever he was hiding was probably from his past, wouldn't you think? Something he didn't want his wife to find out about?"

"Possibly." Joe made the word stretch over several seconds. "But how do you know he wasn't having an affair?"

"Um. . .well. . . ." I knew Joe wouldn't question that I got my information from He Who Waits, but I still didn't know how to say it aloud. My hesitation must have given him the answers he needed.

"Okay, so you know he wasn't having an affair. Anything else come to you while we were talking with her?"

"No. Sorry."

Joe looked disappointed.

"Nothing except what I told you earlier, but that wasn't while we were talking with Ellen."

He nodded. "Well, I guess we should let her get back to her business here, shouldn't we?"

It sounded cold and heartless to me, but Joe was definitely more used to dealing with the harsher realities of his job than I was. It wasn't a quality I was ready to cultivate in my own life. Another reason why I'd rather keep my mysteries in book form.

"I'll tell you what," Joe began, interrupting my thoughts, "why don't you go hang out in the break room while I finish up with Ellen? I'll get her an escort to the morgue—someone who can help her make arrangements to transport her husband's body home for burial."

I nodded. The emotional toll it had taken in meeting with the widow left me drained and with a deep urge to call Matt. I asked Joe where the break room was and, after he pointed the way, headed down the hall, grateful to spend the next few minutes alone sorting out my thoughts and emotions.

One step into the sparse room, however, and all hope of solitude fled.

Chapter Twenty-Eight

The break room was large, sparse, and cool. Two round tables were surrounded by uncomfortable looking plastic chairs that had seen better days more than a decade ago. A vending machine was flanked on either side by soda machines. The Formica countertop was chipped and dirty. A few empty coffee mugs stood in the sink, and a dozen more sat in a drying rack. The coffee pot on the counter was cold and the remaining coffee looked as if it had been there for hours. A refrigerator and a bulletin board—both covered in various announcements—rounded out the decor.

In the center of the room stood He Who Waits.

"You did well, *Cuwitku*. Your presence provided comfort to the grieving woman."

I shrugged, not convinced the compliment was appropriate considering the pain facing Ellen Mesmer. "Not sure it was enough."

The shaman nodded tersely. "It is difficult to provide comfort for people you do not know. Though you may think you spoke only words, to the *wiwazica*, your words were a light of hope for her dark soul."

Wiwazica was a new word to me. It didn't mean woman, so I guessed it meant widow. Whatever the word meant, I understood who He Who Waits was referring to.

"I still don't think it was enough. I know she's grieving. I know I would be a mess if something happened to Matt."

He Who Waits nodded. "You should talk to him. Never let a moment pass where you do not tell those you love how important they are."

As he spoke the last words, I found myself alone in the break room

"Thank you," I whispered, knowing my spirit guide was never truly too far away to hear me. As I reached for my phone and called home, I consoled myself with the knowledge that I'd be able to hug and kiss Matt and the kids within a few hours. The emotional toil of the last interview brought me close to tears. Add grief counselor to the list of jobs I never wanted.

Upon hearing Matt's voice, a flood of emotion threatened to overtake me: relief that I could talk with him, amazement at our life together so far, love for the man I planned to spend my life with. I was so overwhelmed that, for a moment, I couldn't speak.

"Cer? You okay? Cerri?"

I inhaled deeply, trying to keep my emotions in check. The last thing I wanted to do was have my voice crack. If it did, I wasn't sure the emotions could easily be bottled back up. Crying my eyes out at the FBI office—even if it was only in the break room—didn't seem like a good idea. Once I got my voice under control, I said, "Yeah, I'm here. I'm fine. I just…just wanted to tell you that I love you."

"I love you, too. Are you sure you're okay?" In the background I could hear the kids talking to each other. It sounded like they were excited about something.

"I'm fine. Honest." Another deep breath and I could feel my emotions back on a more even keel. "Joe and I just got done talking with the widow and I really wanted to check in. To make sure you know how much I love you."

"Thanks, honey. That's sweet."

Since I wasn't normally so emotional, I could tell Matt wasn't sure how to take it. I opted for changing the subject to put us both more at ease. "How's everything going?"

"Fine." Matt stretched the word out more than necessary, which meant either he didn't believe me or he was preparing to tell me something I wouldn't like. I opted for the latter.

"What's going on?"

"The kids and I are going on an outing. A field trip."

My left eyebrow rose of its own accord. "A field trip? Where?"

"The Classic." He almost whispered the phrase.

After my experience around the Black Hills Motorcycle Classic, I wasn't sure I wanted the kids roaming the streets, even in daylight. Before I had a chance to say anything, though, Matt continued.

"We're not actually going into the town. Zach's friend Cory or Cody—"

"Cody."

"Right. Cody. Anyway, his mom called and said there's a motocross race up near the classic. Cody is racing and wanted to know if Zach wanted to come watch."

My mothering instincts were instantly on alert. "Uh huh."

"Sounded like fun, so we're going to go to the track. It's on the south side of the interstate. You've seen it, right?"

"Uh huh."

"It'll be fun. Zach's really looking forward to it."

I couldn't keep quiet any longer. "You're not going to let him race, are you?"

"No. I promise. We're just going to watch."

"Uh huh." It wasn't that I didn't trust my husband. I just knew that he could be easily persuaded by the angelic faces of our children.

"Honey."

Ouch. I knew that tone. It was the "don't you trust me with our own children" tone that ripped the fabric of my soul. Of course I trusted him. He just wasn't the mother.

I spoke none of this. Instead I replied, "Go. Have a good time. Be careful. I love you."

In the background I heard Zach ask, "Dad, can we take the video camera? That would be so cool!" I could picture him jumping up and down in his excitement.

"Sure. Go get the bag," Matt replied. To me he said, "Cerri, I gotta go. Do you think you can meet us up there? I'll have my phone."

I told Matt I would try to find a way to meet him and the kids, though I wasn't sure how that would work. It wasn't until after we hung up that I began to worry about the details, the most pressing one being how I was going to find a way to the track. Joe had picked me up, so I didn't have a vehicle. The Black Hills Motorcycle Classic was held at least twenty miles to the west and hitchhiking—even around the block—would never be an option for me. I was just too paranoid.

I put my elbows on the table and lowered my head into my hands, rubbing my temples with my thumbs. I could feel a stress headache trying to take hold.

Frankly, I had too much to do to be stuck in the FBI's break room. I could have been working on a recipe review I was doing for a cooking magazine, or even the Bear Butte article I hadn't bothered to officially accept yet. The house could use some tidying. Laundry needed to be done and I'd really hoped to take the kids to the library this week. All of which was more important to me than sitting in the break room waiting.

Or I just didn't want to be near Ellen's understandably raw grief any more.

Or I was just plain tired.

And sitting in an office was not going to convince Matt that motocross was a bad idea for our only son. Or a puppy was too much work for any of us.

A chuckle pulled me out of my self-pity. I knew He Who Waits hadn't gone far.

"The problems of parents do not truly change."

I looked at the shaman. His light tan pants and shirt were adorned with tiny, multi-colored beads in intricate designs. I had no idea if He Who Waits had ever been more than a spirit, let alone if he'd fathered children, but I was fairly certain he'd never discussed the merits of dirt bikes.

Before I could verbalize my thoughts, however, He Who Waits continued. "A sleeker pony. A faster vehicle. A prettier dress. A nicer doll. Children want it all because they do not know what they want."

I nodded, understanding the truth in what my spirit guide was saying.

"Your children will be blessed with your guidance. However, there is another child who will not have such blessing. You must find justice."

Robert's son, Chase.

Opening my mouth, I began to ask how, but He Who Waits had vanished again.

"Well, that certainly wasn't helpful," I said aloud.

"I wouldn't say that." Joe's voice startled me from behind.

Turning around in my chair, I asked, "What?"

The quizzical expression on Joe's face lasted only a second. "You said it wasn't helpful. I disagree. I think you did a great job."

"Oh, um, thanks." I didn't feel right accepting the praise, but that seemed better than admitting that I was talking to myself. Or to a spirit guide, which seemed weird. Clearly, I was never going to be completely comfortable discussing the hocus-pocus stuff that seemed to be colliding with my otherwise normal life.

However, false praise was the least of my worries or frustration. I needed to get to the classic. Well, maybe not the classic, but between the mystery of Robert's death and the heartbreak I felt from Ellen, I needed to spend time with my husband and kids to recharge. Maybe some time away would help me see things clearer.

"…will drive you back and then he'll meet me up at the classic. Does that work for you?" Joe stared at me expectantly.

I could feel the deer in the headlights look as it occurred to me that I had no idea what the FBI agent was talking about.

"In your own little world, huh?" Joe asked.

I nodded, but remained silent. Feeling my embarrass-sment coloring my cheeks.

"Anything that might be helpful?"

"Not that I can think of. Really. I'm just not sure how much help I really am this time. Sorry." I wasn't sure why I was apologizing, but it felt like something I should do. Then again, it wasn't like I had asked to be a part of this investigation.

"Don't sweat it," Joe replied, shrugging. "Anyway, I was saying that one of the victim's advocates is escorting Mrs. Mesmer to the morgue and will stay with her while she gets all that straightened out. My buddy the park ranger is on his way here to drop some reports off. He offered to take you back home and I'm going to head up to the classic and check out a lead there."

"Actually, Matt and the kids are headed to the classic." I explained what was going on and asked Joe if I could tag along.

He agreed and the two of us made our way to his waiting vehicle.

Chapter Twenty-Nine

The multitude of motorcycles made Interstate 90 seem louder and more crowded than I'd remembered even from a few days ago. My anxiety rose with the rumble of the bikes and knowing I was heading in the direction of my family did nothing to alleviate my tension.

I felt like a toddler on the verge of a temper tantrum.

Joe must have sensed my mood because he didn't try to talk with me during the half-hour drive. At least not until we got closer to the town.

"Where are you meeting Matt?" Joe's voice was a blend of professionalism and compassion.

"The race track. But I don't know how to get there." Although a number of bikes had gone east and just as many seemed to be heading west, the traffic situation rivaled any of California's freeways during rush hour.

"Don't sweat it. I do." Joe pointed to a huge hill on the south side of the interstate. "You know where at the race to meet him?"

"I didn't expect it to be so busy." Main Street had been full, but the hill seemed to hold a multitude more people. Dirt tracks climbed their way from bottom to top and spectators stood in mobs so tight it looked like a continuous flow. I grabbed my phone before continuing. "I'll text him and find out where to meet. By the looks of it, between the crowd and the bikes, he probably won't hear the phone ring if I called him and even if he did, a conversation would be tough."

Out of the corner of my eye, I saw Joe nod as I sent Matt a quick text letting him know I was almost at the race track and asking where we should meet.

Matt hadn't replied by the time Joe got to the track's entrance. It took a few minutes of reassuring, but the FBI Agent reluctantly dropped me off and left in pursuit of his own lead. With any luck his clue would pan out and I could go back to my normal life. Whatever that was.

163

Once inside the confines of the arena, I began to scour faces looking for my husband or children. Less than five minutes past before I thought I must have looked at close to five hundred faces and really only wanted to see one that was slightly familiar. Matt still hadn't responded to my text so I sent it again, wondering how families ever found each other in a crowd before cell phones.

I didn't want to venture far from the track entrance. With the crowds entering and leaving the track, though, I couldn't hang out at the gate. However, I didn't know where Matt and the kids were, let alone where Zach's friend Cody and his mother, Jolee, were. I wanted to look through my phone to see if I had Jolee's number, and I wasn't coordinated enough to do that while mulling through a crowd. I wasn't coordinated to look at my phone and walk through an empty room.

A few feet away, I spied a garbage can. Thinking it would be a good place to at least wait, I made my way toward it, trying not to bump into anyone.

Standing next to a garbage can in August's heat, however, was not a good idea. The stench of rotting garbage hit me before I reached my destination.

I checked my phone again. Still no word from Matt.

Taking in my surroundings, I searched for another spot to use as a meet-up location. There was nothing near the gate and the crowds gave no intention of thinning out.

A little further in, however, there seemed to be booths. I figured they would sell drinks and food, and possibly t-shirts and other Black Hills Motorcycle Classic memorabilia. Above the steady murmur of the crowd and the hum of the racing motorcycles, I could make out a voice over a loudspeaker. Where there was a loudspeaker, there was a person talking, and probably a lost and found or something similar where I could ask them to have Matt meet me.

Having decided upon a course of action, I began to move with the crowd. I was able to relax a little and noticed there were a number of vendors lining the main thoroughfare. The set up reminded me of a fair, with ample walking space with booths lining each side: here someone selling t-shirts, there a lemonade stand, even further a booth that had motorcycle accessories.

Now that I had a plan, I felt more comfortable browsing through some of the booths as I passed. I kept my phone in my left hand, hoping that I'd feel the vibrations if Matt called or texted me back. With the noise of the crowd, hearing my ringtone was out of the question.

The first booth I stopped at had clothing items of all types and sizes with the official logo of the Black Hills Motorcycle Classic. I toyed with the thought of getting a t-shirt, before dismissing the idea.

As I followed the crowd further in, I continued to scan the sea of people for familiar faces.

Further up, I was again forced to a standstill. I had hoped that the throng of people would have dispersed more, but that didn't seem to be the case. Any place connected to the classic suffered from a case of perpetual overcrowding. I was reminded again that the popularity of the classic forced the population of a major destination stuffed into the infrastructure of a sleepy town for the week.

I didn't want to get too far from the main gate. I hadn't noticed a lost-and-found or announcement booth or even any security, but I knew those things had to be close by. The edge of the crowd was only a few feet away and I made my way toward the closest booth to try and get some space and give me time to scout out someone who might be able to make an announcement for me.

"Cerri!" Someone called my name, but I didn't see who. I didn't recognize the voice and assumed whoever yelled meant *Carrie*. It was an easy enough mistake to make.

I kept walking with the crowd, still looking for a security guard, or a lost and found booth, or someone who might look like they could help. Deep down I felt a little ridiculous, as well. I knew the kids were fine with Matt. It was their mother who was lost.

The mass of people started to disperse and I made my way toward one of the vendor booths nearby. Looking ahead, there didn't seem to be any type of "Lost Mom" area, and I was hoping that someone in the nearby booth could at least point me in the right direction.

Reaching the table, I found a booth for a custom-built motorcycle business, but couldn't tell which business. Since I didn't see a public address system behind the tables, my first thought was to head back toward the main gate where I might be able to find someone with a walkie-talkie. However, once I was out of sun, beneath the canvas awning covering the booth, my intentions could wait. Even though there wasn't an additional breeze, just being out of the direct sun made me feel cooler. Not having the sun beat on my head was worth the delay in finding Matt and the kids in the crowd.

I checked my phone again, but there was still no message from Matt. "Dang it."

"I'm sorry, are you looking for something?" Looking up from my phone, I saw a man looking at me expectantly. "Can I help you find something?"

I hadn't realized I'd spoken aloud and I quickly lowered my eyes in embarrassment. I could feel my cheeks warming despite the shade. "Um, just looking. Thanks."

I re-sent the text to Matt—again—but didn't think I'd get an answer. At this point I was hoping that by re-sending the message he'd figure out his phone was going off. Even as far away from the track as I was, everything was loud. I could almost feel my heart beat changing to match the ebb and flow of the motorcycles on the track. The smell of dust combined with the noise to convince me I wasn't far from the action. With all the people and noise, finding Matt and the kids would be like finding a needle in a haystack. My best bet was going to be to head back to the gate and either find a security guard who had to be around somewhere, hope to see them when they left the races, or spot the car and wait there. I wasn't fond of my choices, but I didn't see that I had any other options.

After resting for a moment, trying to collect my thoughts, I began to look at the merchandise decorating the booth I'd stopped at. Handlebars and saddlebags acted as focal points, while photo albums and brochures filled the tables. To the side and behind the tables stood motorcycles in various sizes. To my left, a man and boy about Zach's age were studying a miniature bike that would have made my son green with envy.

Without meaning to eavesdrop, I heard the child peppering the

166

adult with questions about the machine. "Is it fast? Would I get a driver's license? Did Grandma really let you have one when you were my age?"

The adult laughed and began answering the boy's questions as they walked toward other bikes. Their conversation reminded me again of Zach's sudden interest in motocross and I was tempted to follow the pair in an effort to hear what the man said to the child, hoping his answers would put me more at ease about my own son wanting a bike.

"Are you sure I can't help you?" The man who'd spoken to me earlier asked again.

I shrugged. "My son is interested in…" I waved my hand around the booth. "This stuff. But I don't know the first thing about motorcycles or dirt bikes or, well, any of that."

The man nodded his understanding and I took a moment to study his features. He looked familiar, but I wasn't sure why. Then again, with all the faces I'd been searching recently, it's possible he had walked passed me at some point and I recognized him from that brief encounter. The man started explaining about ccs and strokes, but he could have been speaking Ancient Hebrew for all I understood. My face must have expressed my bewilderment.

He chuckled and ran what looked like a handkerchief over his bald head. "You really don't know much about bikes, do you?"

I shook my head, but didn't speak.

"Okay, let's start over. I'm Vic." He held out his hand, which I gladly shook. His strong grip didn't surprise me, given the size of his biceps. What did surprise me was his friendliness, despite the "hardcore biker" image he portrayed from a distance. Once again I was reminded that things aren't always what they seem.

"Cerri. Nice to meet you. And you're right, I have no idea about bikes. I can barely tell the difference between a ten-speed and a motorcycle."

Vic asked a few questions and began to explain how motocross bikes worked.

I tried to pay attention, but had difficulty. I kept alternating between looking at the pedestrian walkway to see if my family was nearby and glancing at my phone to see if Matt finally replied to my text messages. Since the subject of motorbikes was over my head anyway, I found it even harder to concentrate, which made me clumsy.

After the third time I dropped my cell phone, I finally stuck the devise in my back pocket, hoping I'd feel the vibration when Matt texted. I thought about throwing the phone in my purse, but I knew I'd never hear it once it hit the black hole of my handbag.

I wasn't happy about the prospect of not knowing if Matt tried calling me, or the possibility of having to pay for a taxi all the way home, but losing my phone meant I would be completely stranded. And I was sure Matt wouldn't leave without calling. He knew I was planning to meet him and the kids here.

"...is your son?" Vic's words took my focus away from my phone, but I didn't know what he'd actually asked.

"I'm sorry. Could you repeat that?"

"I asked 'how old is your son?'. We have bikes for all ages and abilities. It would really be best if your son were here so we could fit him to just the right bike."

I shrugged and nodded simultaneously. "Well, he's here somewhere. I keep expecting to hear from my husband." I reached to my back pocket and pulled out my phone, checking again for messages. I must have had one of Joe's business cards in my pocket because it was attached to my phone's screen. I removed the card to see a continuing lack of messages.

Vic didn't seem fazed by my distracted attitude and went on to discuss the virtues of various bikes. "... and this one has a slightly touchier throttle. All of our bikes are custom made and the frames on these are very light. Perfect for a beginner."

As I listened, I realized Vic had an accent, but it was faint and I couldn't quite place it. "A custom-made bike for motocross is probably far out of my price range. Thank you, though. I appreciate you taking the time to explain the bikes to me."

I turned to walk away, thinking I'd head toward the main gate again. A hand on my arm stopped me.

I jerked my arm back as I whipped around to face Vic. "What the—"

He quickly held up both hands. "Whoa! Sorry. I just wanted to show you one more thing. Please? Plus I have some catalogues I'd like to give you."

He sounded contrite, and I felt bad for overreacting. "Um, yeah. Sure."

Vic smiled and motioned for me to follow him. We headed further into the booth, away from the crowded promenade toward an enclosed, custom-built trailer similar to the ones I'd seen all over the Black Hills hauling motorcycles. This one was the size of a horse trailer and was parked parallel to the main walkway. It was painted red with "Bone's Bikes" scripted on the side and a decorated skull featured prominently beneath the words.

I glanced back at the throngs of people before following Vic to the rear of the trailer where there was a real door allowing people to get in and out without having to lower the back ramp. He opened the door and motioned for me to enter. "This will just take a minute," he said.

Once inside, he shut the metal door quickly and produced a knife. Where it came from, I couldn't tell, but even from a distance I could tell it was sharp.

I didn't have much time to dwell on the knife, though, since Vic pushed me into the wall of the trailer. Hard.

Chapter Thirty

I must have been knocked out, because the next thing I knew I was waking up with my ankles duct taped together, my hands secured behind me and something sticky covering my mouth. The dull grey color I could see on my cheek made me believe it was duct tape. I wanted to gag. My head was throbbing and my back ached. I thought I felt something wet and sticky on my head, and hoped it was sweat rather than blood.

I could tell I was still in the trailer, which had been converted to a part office-part mechanics shop. The office took up less than a third of the space and I'd been left behind the three-foot long desk, my knees up to my chin and nowhere to move in my bound and gagged state.

The air inside was stale and unmoving, making it hotter than it had been outside. I tried to hear the crowds or the motorcycle races but couldn't. I wasn't sure if the races had already ended or if the trailer had blocked out the noise. Either way, I assumed if I couldn't hear noises outside, no one was probably around to hear any noise I made inside the trailer, either.

"Boy, you really got yourself in a mess, didn't ya?"

I turned my head toward the voice, and was immediately rewarded with a sharp pain in my head. It took a minute for my eyes to focus, but I saw Bill the green fairy buzzing near my nose. I tried to tell him to get help, but it sounded more like "memh memp."

"I have no idea what you just said, but I'm guessing you'd like some help."

Slowly, to avoid more pain, I nodded.

He shrugged. "Sorry. I already tried. I can't get that tape stuff off your face."

Tears that had been welling up, spilled down my cheeks. I had no idea exactly where I was or how long I'd been there or if anyone knew I was missing. And I couldn't even ask.

"Hey, hey, don't cry." Bill looked worried, as if he'd never seen a woman cry before and didn't know how to handle the emotions. "Please. Help is on the way. I think."

I sniffled and looked at the fairy with an expression that I hoped conveyed all my questions.

"Vesta went to get help, although I'm not really sure how that's going to work, since most humans don't believe in us, let alone listen to what we say."

Vesta? The snotty fairy with no use for humans was trying to get me some help? Great.

"Anyway, she and I found you here and she offered to get help. I think she has an idea, but she took off so quickly that I didn't ask."

Even better. She probably went home.

"Right after she left, your phone went crazy. It started shaking and making weird noises." Bill shrugged. "I dunno what all. Well, I think it was your phone. Either that or your pants make weird noises." The fairy laughed.

I tried moving a little, and verified that my phone was still in my back pocket. Moving was difficult and I was sore, but the throbbing pain had subsided a little. I prayed that was a good sign.

My phone went off again and I tried to reach it with my hands bound behind me, but I couldn't. The realization brought another round of tears to my eyes.

Bill noticed. "Whoa! Don't start that again."

As much as I wanted to cry since I couldn't do anything else, I took a few deep breaths and managed to calm down. The last thing I wanted was to be left completely alone and Bill was at least a distraction. I wondered where He Who Waits was and why he hadn't shown up to get me out of this mess.

"Good. You don't look like you're gonna cry again. Anyway, your phone was going crazy so someone must be missing you. If they're missin' ya, they're lookin' for ya."

I couldn't argue with his logic even if I'd wanted to.

"I guess you also figured out that the person who killed your friend works for Bone's Bikes, huh? But why didn't you bring one of your police to arrest the bad guy?"

Around the time I saw the knife I had a pretty good idea who had killed Robert Mesmer, but until then I had been clueless. I wanted to tell the fairy that Robert hadn't been my friend—that I'd never met him—and I still didn't know exactly why he had to die. I remained silent since I had no other option. I took another deep breath to try and calm myself down.

"...So that's when we figured it out. And we went looking for you and saw you follow him. That wasn't very smart, was it? And you shoulda seen that guy when he went through your bag. You really shouldn't have had that drawing of him in it. It kinda stinks in here, don't it?"

While Bill paused for air, I considered what he'd said. A drawing of Vic? At first, I couldn't think of any drawing I would have had of the man, then I remembered the one I'd gotten from Judy and Brittany. I must not have given the picture to Joe, but it did explain why I thought Vic looked familiar. Slowly I turned my head and found the contents of my purse dumped onto the floor; the sketch in question crumpled into a ball a few feet away.

That explained why I was bound. Vic must have thought I was on to him instead of realizing I was an idiot with bad luck. If only Matt had answered his phone, I wouldn't be in this mess. I took another deep breath and pushed the thought out of my head. Blaming Matt for not hearing his phone with all the noise around was ridiculous. He probably couldn't even hear his own thoughts.

Now that I was thinking of Matt, I wondered if he had even missed me yet. I hoped so. Then again, he probably had no idea where to even look for me.

I tried to focus my attention back on Bill, who was still talking and flitting around from one spot to the other. I wondered if he was full of nervous energy or if fairies had to continue to move like hummingbirds did.

"...and she should be back soon. I don't think she would have gone too far, but sometimes it's hard to get humans to notice, ya know?" Bill stopped a few inches from my head. "It really smells funny in here. Don't you think so?"

He was right. There were some smells I associated with cars— oil, gasoline, sweat—and some I associated with the races going on

172

nearby—dirt, exhaust. Somewhere the scent of tobacco was added to the mix as well as a grassy smell that reminded me of rotting alfalfa. Bill was right; the combination smelled funny.

I started to nod when Bill zipped close to my ear. "Quiet. Don't move. Someone's coming."

A bang on the side of the trailer punctuated his words and I jumped in spite of myself.

Chapter Thirty-One

A door at the far end of the trailer opened, but I couldn't see who entered. Boxes of what I suspected were motorcycle parts were stacked up between the office area and the rest of the trailer, blocking any view I would have had over the office desk.

"In here." I recognized Vic's voice from earlier.

"You keep the stuff here? Whatever," came another man's voice. It was familiar, but I couldn't place where I might have heard it before.

Then again, maybe I was grasping at straws.

Footsteps came closer and I tried to make myself as small as possible. From around one of the boxes, I saw Vic's face. "Don't make a sound," he mouthed. The murderous look on his face would have deterred me, even if I hadn't been scared to death.

He turned around and grabbed one of the boxes, carrying it back toward the door. "It's in here."

The other man grunted. "How much for a packet?"

Packet? I didn't know much about motorcycles, but I didn't think any parts came in packets.

"$25 per," came Vic's terse reply.

"Three grams?"

Grams? Packet? Was Vic a drug dealer besides a murdering kidnapper?

"Yep. I'll give you a discount if you want to buy bulk. This is some of the best spice out there. Most states don't even have laws against it yet." Vic's laugh held no humor.

The two men continued talking in hushed tones about quantities and cost while my mind tried to wrap around everything going on around me. Probably since I was trying so hard to be silent, it seemed like my hearing had reached superhero proportions. None of what the two men said, however, made any sense to me.

I sat as quietly as I could, trying to calm my breathing. Every breath I took sounded like a tornado and my heart was beating like a freight train. Surly Vic and his drug buddy could hear it. Thoughts like those didn't help and I was finding it more and more difficult to remain perfectly still and equally quiet.

The flies landing on me didn't help matters. In fact, they were grossing me out. I wanted to move to get them off, but I was too afraid of making noise. I closed my eyes, I could feel tears starting to well up.

My thoughts turned to Matt and the kids. I prayed for the opportunity to see them again. I shivered, despite trying to remain perfectly still. I couldn't allow myself to think that way.

I concentrated on the conversation going on a few feet away. Since the mystery man's voice sounded familiar to me, I struggled to remember where I'd heard it. I came up empty.

"When are you pulling out?" the mystery man asked.

"Dunno," Vic replied. "Monday probably. Tuesday at the latest. Why?"

"In case I need more. You got more, right?"

"Yeah. I got plenty. And this is a good mix. Like I said, most states don't have laws against it. Hell, you can buy stuff that ain't this good in convenience stores just about anywhere."

The mystery man grunted.

At that moment, my phone rang.

For a moment, I froze. Then I tried to reach the phone, still in my back pocket, but my bound hands made it impossible without moving and making even more noise. All the while I prayed that the men hadn't heard it ring.

"What was that?" the mystery man asked.

"I guess one of the guys left their phone on the desk back there," Vic answered tersely. "Now, do you want this stuff or not?"

"Yeah. I'll take two. I can find you at the campground if I need more, right?"

"Yeah. That'll be fifty."

"Here. Hey, do you know where I can get a good hot dog with just mustard?"

Then things got really crazy.

175

Chapter Thirty-Two

As soon as the mystery man finished speaking, I heard the loudest noise I ever imagined. A combination of banging and yelling and cursing seemed to come from every direction.

One word I heard loud and clear, though. "Police!"

I started making as much noise as possible.

It didn't take long for an officer to find me.

The next few hours were a blur of activity. Kind of.

Officers removed the duct tape from my mouth, hands, and ankles and took me to Rapid City Regional Hospital to be evaluated, even though I said I was fine. Frankly, I just wanted to go home and hug my husband and children.

While I was waiting at the hospital, I heard a familiar voice coming from the hallway making my heart skip a beat.

"I want to see my wife." Matt sounded worried and agitated. I wondered how much he'd been told.

Seconds later, the door to the hospital room opened. I'd never been so glad to see someone.

I jumped off the bed and ran to Matt, who enveloped me in his arms. I didn't want the hug to ever end.

When we finally tore ourselves apart, I noticed Joe standing in the doorway. He seemed uncomfortable at witnessing the moment, but didn't speak.

"How did you know where to find me?" I asked, not caring which man answered.

It was Matt who spoke, his voice cracking with emotions. "I finally checked my phone when you still hadn't shown up. I'm so sorry. I should have checked it earlier. Can you forgive me?"

I nodded, not trusting myself to speak because of my own emotions. He didn't need me to break down in relief just yet.

"And I should have listened to Kenzie. She said you needed help. I just didn't understand what she was talking about." Matt paused. "Honestly, I thought she was bored and making stuff up. I mean, she said the fairy told her. Kids say the weirdest things, don't they?"

The fairy. Vesta must have found Kenzie and tried to warn my daughter. I made a note to give Kenzie an extra hug for her efforts and another pink ribbon for the cantankerous fairy.

"Strange," I replied. "But that doesn't explain how you knew I was at the hospital."

"I can answer that," Joe said. "When Matt couldn't get ahold of you, he called me. I told him that I'd dropped you off at the race track. By that time, I was actually done with my interview, so I headed back."

Matt picked up the story from there. "The kids and I walked down toward the entrance, but there were cops everywhere diverting foot traffic, so we had to go another way. When we finally got the main gate, you weren't there, either, but Joe was. Jolee and Cody—you remember Zack's friend and his mom—were with us. She offered to take the kids out for pizza and then back to her house. I still wasn't sure how to find you and I was imagining all kinds of terrible things." A look of anguish crossed his face, quickly replaced by relief. "But you're okay. You are okay."

He hugged me again before continuing. "Anyway, right before she got in the car, Kenzie ran back and said 'Find Mommy. Use the Brat Finder. Mommy needs us.' I still didn't understand what she meant."

"But I did," Joe interrupted. "You have the Brat Finder app on your phone, don't you?"

I nodded. I'd been playing with some of the free phone apps and found one that was designed to keep track of children. Even though the kids were too young to have phones of their own, I was curious how the GPS enabled app worked and wanted to play with it. I thought it would help me find my phone if I'd ever misplaced it, even though it was designed to keep track of children. I couldn't remember telling either Matt or the kids that I'd downloaded it, though.

"That's a smart kid. She's a lot like her mom, isn't she?" Joe's question told me he wasn't dismissing Kenzie's fairy tale.

"I do have some pretty smart kids, don't I?" I replied, leaving

177

Joe's real question unanswered.

Matt picked up the story again. "Since Joe knew what that app was, we used it to find you. Although, I'll admit, I did try calling and texting a bunch of times before we found you. Anyway, Joe said that it showed your phone was here so here we are." Matt paused. "When he told me you were at the hospital…"

"I'm okay. I'm really okay." I tried reassuring Matt, but I could tell it would take a long time before he believed I really was fine.

Joe spoke again. "When we got here, I saw an officer I knew and was able to get some of the details. However, he did tell me you would need to go for a debriefing. The task force is a little confused about how you ended up in the trailer. But I think Karl—or Frank, rather—can help clear that up."

I nodded, then winced in pain. In my relief, at seeing Matt, I hadn't noticed how sore my arms and legs were from being bound. But at least now I knew why the mystery man's voice had seemed so familiar in the trailer. It must have been Joe's undercover friend.

"Are you okay?" Matt asked.

"Just sore. I'll be fine after a hot bath."

At that moment, the door opened again and a doctor walked in followed by a man I had never seen before. The mystery man carried an air of confidence that made me assume he was law enforcement of some type.

"Mrs. Baker," the doctor began. "You seem to be fine. There doesn't seem to be any concussion. You may have some bruising, and you'll probably be stiff and sore for a few days. I'm going to prescribe some muscle relaxers if you need them and then we'll go ahead and release you."

The other man made a noise as if to clear his throat.

The doctor only glanced at him and shrugged. "I'll get the paperwork started." With that, the doctor turned to leave.

"Agent Oliver, you may handle the debrief. We need a statement as to what she heard," said the mystery man as soon as the hospital room door clicked closed. "Mr. Baker. Mrs. Baker."

He left without another word.

I looked at Joe and Matt, confused as to what exactly had

happened. Matt looked as bewildered as I was.

Joe shrugged. "Let's get you out of here and then I'll try to explain everything."

The nurse showed up then and I filled out the paperwork required to leave the hospital.

I tried not to dwell on how the day could have ended.

Chapter Thirty-Three

Matt wouldn't let go of my hand as we exited the building.

"Matt, she needs to come with me," Joe said quietly.

"She didn't do anything wrong." Matt's words were terse, and I knew he was worried.

"It's okay, honey. I'll answer Joe's questions. Make a statement. Then they can put that creep behind bars." I leaned up to kiss Matt's cheek. "Besides I have a few questions of my own."

Matt nodded, but said nothing as he disentangled his fingers from mine. To Joe he said, "You'll bring her home? Safely."

"You have my word."

The two men shook hands, but it seemed forced on Matt's part. I knew it would be a long time before he would let me out of his sight for any length of time.

Matt headed toward our car, while Joe steered me toward his.

"You didn't ride together," I asked.

Joe shook his head. "No. As soon as we knew you were at the hospital, Matt took off. I figured he'd need some time to cool off, anyway. I know he's worried. I'm sorry."

"It wasn't your fault. I'm not even sure exactly how this all happened."

Joe only nodded as we got into his car. Neither of us spoke again until we were at the FBI Headquarters.

Once inside, Joe found an interview room and got us both some water. He asked me to relay everything that happened from the time he dropped me off until I arrived at the hospital. Repeatedly. I think I told him the entire story three or four times.

When he was finally satisfied with my statement, he had me write everything down that I'd just told him before we left the interview room and headed toward Joe's car.

"I think I have the rest of it figured out," I said as we got into the car.

"Go ahead. I'll let you know if you're wrong," he said. "If I can, that is."

"Well," I began, "obviously, Vic was selling drugs."

"Right. K-2 to be precise. It's a synthetic marijuana-type drug that causes a lot of damage. Like those bath salts that were in the news a few years ago. It's a lot more dangerous than the natural version. And he is part of a pretty big operation, which is why a task force had been sent."

I nodded. "When I was talking to him about motocross bikes, I had pulled my phone out of my pocket and one of your cards had been stuck to the phone. He must have seen that and thought I was on to him."

"As near as we can tell, yes."

"After he knocked me out by slamming me into the side of the trailer, he must have gone through my purse and found the sketch I got from the girls who saw Robert fighting with him at the campground. I didn't figure that out until I had woken up and saw the sketch crumpled in the corner and my purse dumped onto the floor." I took a deep breath. "But what I don't understand is what he had to do with Robert. I mean, Vic killed Robert, right?"

The idea that there was still a murderer loose sent shivers down my spine.

"We think so, yes," came Joe's reply. "Based on what you found out, Vic was definitely the guy who argued with Robert before he was killed. He's admitted to it, even. After I dropped you off at the races, I talked with Detective McShane again. You had mentioned that the killer came from LA, and it occurred to me that the postal abbreviation for Louisiana is LA."

"I should have realized that," I said. "I guess I was so excited about having a lead for you that I didn't think that the—my source would talk in riddles." I still wouldn't admit to the FBI Agent that I got information from fairies.

Joe shrugged. "Well, I talked with McShane and he confirmed a few other things. Around the time Ellen said Robert became more agitated, Robert's mother had died. That's where that money had been going. McShane had actually talked with the mother a few times over the years and had a feeling that Robert tried to stay out of trouble. She often called him a good son, but family can be pretty biased."

181

"That explains why there wasn't even a parking ticket for him then, doesn't it? He was trying extra hard to stay out of trouble."

"Probably. Anyway, I also looked through the file the Shreveport police sent and found one other thing. Vic and the kid killed then were not only in the same gang, but they were also step brothers."

I nodded. "So Vic wanted revenge and waited decades to get it."

"Looks that way," Joe replied. "One thing we're not sure about is why here? Why now? And why did Robert think Vic would give up—not go after him—after the fight at the campground?"

Before I could say "I dunno," He Who Waits materialized in the backseat. My first reaction was to ignore the shaman since he hadn't even kept me company while I was being held hostage in Vic's trailer. My second was to tell him off for the same reason. My third idea won out and I tried to act as normal as possible.

He Who Waits answered Joe, even though the FBI agent couldn't hear the answers. "Robert did not recognize him. Time had not been kind to his former acquaintance."

I relayed the information to Joe, who raised his eyebrow questioningly, but didn't ask how I got the information.

Instead, he said, "Yeah, I imagine it wasn't. That would explain why Robert didn't think that anything more was going to come from that fight. But it must have been when Vic recognized him."

Through the side mirror, I saw He Who Waits nod once.

"And since Robert had decided to ride out to Bear Butte, at a time when not a lot of other people were there, it was a location of opportunity, really."

He Who Waits noiselessly nodded again.

By this time, we'd reached my house and the kids were starting to run toward the car.

Joe and I sat in silence for a few minutes before I spoke again. "I guess that's it. I'm really sorry I wasn't able to be more help." I quickly darted my eyes toward the back seat. "I didn't get as much...extra information as I did before."

"You were more capable. I have told you before that it is your *ozuye* to see justice done," said He Who Waits as he vanished from the vehicle.

Great. Another reminder of my destiny.

Joe and I both got out of the car before he said, "It's okay. I know you tried. And you were a help, even if you don't think so. In fact, I have something for you." Joe pulled an envelope out of his back pocket and handed it to me.

"What's this?" I asked.

A sly smile crept over Joe's face. "Open it."

Inside, I found a check worth more than two freelance writing assignments made out to me. "I don't understand."

By now my family had surrounded us on the driveway, all four of them vying for my attention.

"I talked to my boss, the guy you saw at the hospital, and that's payment for your consulting on this case," Joe said.

Matt glanced at the check and immediately shook Joe's hand.

I was still in shock. "Um, thanks. So I really helped?"

Joe chuckled. "Yes. And by making you an official consultant, it will make it easier for me to share information in the future. If you're willing to help, that is?"

"Sure," I said. "That would be great. I think."

Joe smiled and said he needed to get going and made his way back to his car. Neither Matt nor I spoke until the agent had driven out of sight.

"I'm glad you're home. I'm glad you're safe," Matt said kissing me on the forehead as he gave me a bear hug. "Don't ever scare me like that again."

I kissed his lips. "I won't."

"Mom," Zach interrupted. "Cody said—"

"Not now, Zach," Matt said.

"No, it's okay, honey," I told Matt. "Go ahead, Zach."

"Well, Cody said I could have his old bike. You know, to practice and stuff to see if I really like motocross. Isn't that cool, Mom?"

Cool wasn't the word I would have used, but allowed myself to agree with my son. "Yep, pretty cool. But you be very careful and don't ever ride without telling me or your dad, okay?" I thought I might be able to keep him safe for a little while that way.

Zach nodded, practically jumping up and down in his excitement.

As my family headed back toward the house, Madison stopped and looked at me with a thoughtful expression on her face. "Mommy, Zach gets to keep the bike right?"

"For now." I hoped he wouldn't like motocross.

"You know what that means?" she asked.

"What, honey?"

Madison and Kenzie looked at each other, a grin spreading on their identical faces. "A puppy!"

Matt and I exchanged glances and we all headed back into the house, leaving discussions of bikes and dogs for another day.

Moving is stressfull enough, but when Cerri Baker moves with her family to the Black Hills of South Dakota, she begins see things—things like murder.

Named after a pre-Christian Celtic goddess, Cerri has spent her life trying to avoid the spirituality and the "hocus pocus" her mother embraces. Once in the Black Hills, Cerri doesn't seem to have much choice as her spirit guide insists she find justice for a murdered man. As she struggles with her own destiny, Cerri must also convince the FBI that she is getting her information from another realm and not from first-hand knowledge of the murder.

Ghost Mountain, by Nichole R. Bennett, from Indigo Sea Press, indigoseapress.com